The Miracle Of Birth.

No matter how many times he witnessed it, Tyler was filled with a humbling sense of wonder, as well as a twinge of regret. Since he didn't intend to have children, he'd never have a moment like this to call his own.

This baby boy's father was one hell of a lucky man. And the jerk wasn't even here to realize it.

A mist clouding his eyes, Tyler examined the squirming infant. Ten fingers. Ten toes. He grinned. An impressive sprinkler system.

But as Tyler looked more closely at the boy, his smile faded and the blood drained from his face. A tiny dimple dented the infant's chin, and a telltale cowlick at his forehead parted his thick black hair.

Ty thought back to that night in Chicago. The one and only night he and Lexi had—

He stared in awe at the miracle he held, his gut clenching as realization hit him. The resemblance was more than coincidental. It was undeniable.

Tyler Braden had just delivered his own son.

Dear Reader,

Welcome to the world of Silhouette Desire, where you can indulge yourself every month with romances that can only be described as passionate, powerful and provocative!

Fabulous BJ James brings you June's MAN OF THE MONTH with *A Lady for Lincoln Cade*. In promising to take care of an ex-flame—and the widow of his estranged friend—Lincoln Cade discovers she has a child. Bestselling author Leanne Banks offers another title in her MILLION DOLLAR MEN miniseries with *The Millionaire's Secret Wish*. When a former childhood sweetheart gets amnesia, a wealthy executive sees his chance to woo her back.

Desire is thrilled to present another exciting miniseries about the scandalous Fortune family with FORTUNES OF TEXAS: THE LOST HEIRS. Anne Marie Winston launches the series with *A Most Desirable M.D.*, in which a doctor and nurse share a night of passion that leads to marriage! Dixie Browning offers a compelling story about a sophisticated businessman who falls in love with a plain, plump woman while stranded on a small island in *More to Love*. Cathleen Galitz's *Wyoming Cinderella* features a young woman whose life is transformed when she becomes nanny to the children of her brooding, rich neighbor. And Kathie DeNosky offers her hero a surprise when he discovers a one-night stand leads to pregnancy and true love in *His Baby Surprise*.

Indulge yourself with all six Desire titles—and see details inside about our exciting new contest, "Silhouette Makes You a Star."

Enjoy!

Joan Marlow Golan

Joan Marlow Golan
Senior Editor, Silhouette Desire

Please address questions and book requests to:
Silhouette Reader Service
U.S.: 3010 Walden Ave., P.O. Box 1325, Buffalo, NY 14269
Canadian: P.O. Box 609, Fort Erie, Ont. L2A 5X3

His Baby Surprise
KATHIE DeNOSKY

Published by Silhouette Books
America's Publisher of Contemporary Romance

To Wayne Jordan, for answering my endless questions.

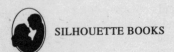 SILHOUETTE BOOKS

ISBN 0-373-76374-3

HIS BABY SURPRISE

Copyright © 2001 by Kathie DeNosky

This edition published by arrangement with Harlequin Books S.A.

® and TM are trademarks of Harlequin Books S.A., used under license.
Trademarks indicated with ® are registered in the United States Patent
and Trademark Office, the Canadian Trade Marks Office and in other
countries.

Visit Silhouette at www.eHarlequin.com

Printed in U.S.A.

Books by Kathie DeNosky

Silhouette Desire

Did You Say Married?! #1296
The Rough and Ready Rancher #1355
His Baby Surprise #1374

KATHIE DeNOSKY

lives in deep Southern Illinois and enjoys dining out, factory outlet malls, traveling through the southern and southwestern states and collecting Native American pottery. After reading and enjoying Silhouette Desire for many years, she is ecstatic about being able to share her stories with others as a Silhouette author. She often starts her day at 2:00 a.m. so she can write without interruption, before the rest of the family is up and about. You may write to Kathie at P.O. Box 2064, Herrin, Il 62948-5264.

One

"**W**hat's wrong now, Martha?" Tyler Braden asked, sighing heavily.

He picked up a patient file from the top of the well-worn counter. In the three days since his arrival in Dixie Ridge, Tennessee, Ty had learned a very important lesson about Nurse Payne. Whatever thoughts she had, she freely shared.

"Are you gonna wear your Sunday-go-to-meetin' clothes every day of the week, Doc?"

Ty opened his lab coat to look down at his white shirt, striped tie and charcoal dress slacks. "What's wrong with the way I'm dressed?"

Martha looked at him over the top of her wire-rimmed glasses as if she thought he might be a bit simpleminded. "Around here, folks don't get gussied up like that unless they're gettin' married or buried."

Ty arched a brow. "What would *you* suggest I wear, Martha?"

She patted the thick, gray bun at the base of her neck—a gesture he'd quickly come to recognize as Martha's preamble to a lecture. When she walked around the counter to stand in front of him, her gaze raking him from head to toe, he had to fight the urge to reach down and make sure his fly was closed. A quick glance south of his belt buckle assured him it was.

"First of all, you need to lose the tie and white shirt. They make you look like you're about to choke." Martha looked thoughtful. "Doc Fletcher wears sports shirts, but you ain't as long in the tooth as Doc, so a T-shirt or sweater would suit you best." She pointed to his crisply pressed slacks, the creases razor sharp. "And while you're at it, you might want to buy yourself some jeans and save those for church." She shrugged. "Course it's up to you. But I'm warnin' you. Folks around here don't care too much for somebody puttin' on airs."

"But I'm not—"

"If you don't want to know, don't ask." Having pronounced judgment, Martha walked back around the counter and picked up the ringing phone. "Dixie Ridge Health Clinic."

Ty bit the inside of his cheek to keep his epithet to himself. When he'd first phoned Dr. Fletcher to discuss temporarily taking over the clinic, the older man had warned him about the crusty nurse.

"Old Martha will be your most valuable asset, but she'll also be your worst critic. Be sure to stay on her good side."

But mere words could never have prepared Ty for

the reality of Martha Payne. With a pleasant, grand-motherly face and the voice of a drill sergeant, she ran the clinic like a well-oiled machine. Serving as both receptionist and nurse, she demonstrated an efficiency that astounded Ty as much as her outspokenness irritated the hell out of him. Since his arrival, he'd been subjected to lectures ranging from his waste of gauze and tape to the appropriate way of answering the clinic phone. Now it appeared her opinions were taking a more personal turn.

Ty had noticed a quiet reserve about the patients. But preoccupied with their symptoms and complaints, he'd assumed it was because they didn't know him. He'd never dreamed it could be because of the clothes he wore. Pulling at the knot of his tie, he yanked it free and stuffed it into the pocket of his lab coat. Thank God, when his six months here were finished, he'd head back to Chicago and not have to listen to Martha reiterate his shortcomings.

Fifteen minutes later Ty bid farewell to Harv Jenkins with a reminder to take his medication regularly, then walked up to the reception counter. "Is that it for the day?"

Martha shook her head and shoved a chart across the counter. "Freddie Hatfield just brought Lexi in. Her water broke and contractions are two minutes apart. She's in the birthin' room and I'd say it won't be too long before it's showtime."

"Has she had any problems during the pregnancy?" Ty asked, scanning the chart. Dr. Fletcher had made few notations aside from the patient's weight and blood pressure.

"Nope. I've known Lexi Hatfield all her life and she's always been as healthy as a horse."

"Has she expressed any concerns about the delivery?"

"Nope." Beaming, Martha rounded the end of the counter. "She's doin' pretty good for a first-timer. But Freddie couldn't get past the front door."

"Nervous wreck?" Ty asked, following Martha down the narrow hall leading to the infirmary.

"Unless it's a matter of life and death, Freddie Hatfield avoids this place like a bachelor avoids a widow's convention." Martha shook her head and laughed. "Always has been delicate. Faints dead away at the smell of antiseptic."

Delicate?

Ty frowned at Martha's description of Fred Hatfield. Of all the terms he thought she might use to describe a man with a weak stomach, delicate wasn't among them.

A low moan from the infirmary broke through his musing. While Martha went to check the patient, Ty entered the locker room to change clothes.

All in all, he'd had a pretty good day, he decided, pulling on the blue scrubs. He hadn't seen anything more serious than Harv Jenkins's sore joints, and anticipated a routine birth.

Rotating his shoulders, Ty found much of the tension that had plagued him in recent weeks had begun to dissipate. Now if he could just get the nightmares under control....

Shaking off the guilt and regret, Ty scrubbed, plastered a smile on his face and shouldered open the door to the birthing room. He wasn't about to let the tragic events that led to his being here intrude on his good mood.

"Where's Freddie?" the patient asked.

Martha laughed. "Where do you think?"

"Over at the Blue Bird."

A tingle raced the length of Ty's spine at the patient's familiar soft southern drawl. Only one woman's voice had ever affected him that way. He glanced over at the bed, but Martha blocked his view. If he didn't know better, he'd swear—

He shook his head at the ridiculous thought.

"Freddie took off out of here like a scalded dog," Martha said.

As he tied the bottom strings of the mask around his neck, Ty listened to the patient groan, then huff and puff her way through a contraction. When it finally eased, she blew out a deep cleansing breath.

"Freddie's a big wimp," she said, her voice raspy.

He couldn't have said it better. No matter how queasy old Fred was, the guy could at least try to be present for the birth of his child.

"O-o-oh, why do they…have to come…so close together?" the woman moaned a split second before she began panting her way through another pain.

His disdain for the weak-kneed Fred increased. Compelled to reassure his patient, Ty walked over to the side of the bed. "You'll do just…"

His voice trailed off as he stared openmouthed at the woman in the final stages of labor. Alexis Madison, popular talk radio hostess and, until almost a year ago, Ty's next door neighbor, was about to give birth in a rural health clinic in eastern Tennessee.

The last time he'd seen Alexis had been the night before she left Chicago. Due to a station buyout, she'd been told to move her show to Los Angeles or find work elsewhere. She'd chosen to quit and move back to Tennessee. In fact, she was one of the reasons he'd taken the job in Dixie Ridge. When he'd been looking for a place to hide from the media, he remembered her talking about the peace and quiet of the Smoky Mountains. After sending out a few feelers, he'd jumped at the chance to temporarily take over the clinic.

The disappointment tightening his chest surprised him. He'd been more than a little attracted to her from the moment they met and had intended to look her up while he was here in the hopes of becoming better acquainted. But there wasn't any reason to do that now. She'd obviously found some guy named Fred as soon as she moved back, gotten married and started a family.

He forced a smile as he gazed down at her. "Hello, Alexis."

Lexi figured it had to be the pain causing hallucinations. It had been almost ten long months since she'd heard Tyler Braden's rich baritone. Besides, the location was all wrong. She was back home in the mountains of Tennessee, not the concrete jungle of Chicago.

But when she opened her eyes, the metallic taste of fear spread through her suddenly dry mouth and she let out a horrified moan. "N-o-o-o…not you!"

"You knew Doc Fletcher wouldn't be here for the delivery," Martha reminded her. She reached up to pat Ty's shoulder. "This here's Doc Braden. He's fillin' in."

Panic swept through Lexi and she grabbed the front of Martha's white uniform. "Get him away from me!"

"Simmer down, Lexi." Martha disengaged herself

and turned to Ty. "Don't take offense. They all act like they're devil possessed by the time they reach this stage of the game."

"Please, Martha," Lexi pleaded. She had to make the woman understand she didn't want Tyler Braden anywhere near her. "I don't want *him* delivering my baby."

"Lexi, you know there ain't another doctor within thirty miles of here," Martha said, her voice stern.

"Then you do it!"

"Now, cut that out." Martha shook her finger. "You know the only time I catch a baby is when the doctor can't get here in time."

"Then go tell Freddie to get the car…and take me to Granny Applegate!" Lexi felt like a beached whale as she struggled to sit up.

"Who the hell is Granny Applegate?" Ty asked.

"An old woman up on Piney Knob," Martha said, pushing Lexi's shoulders back down when she finally managed to prop herself up on her elbows. "Granny takes care of some of the folks around here with her home remedies. And she's delivered more babies than a porcupine has quills or time to count 'em."

Upset and completely unprepared for the next contraction, Lexi moaned. Pain pulled at her insides, demanding her body take action. Closing her eyes, a guttural sound rumbled in the back of her throat as she strained with all her might to push her baby into the world.

When the contraction ended, she opened her eyes to see Ty shaking his head. "Don't be ridiculous, Alexis. There's no other choice. You wouldn't make it as far as the front door before you give birth."

"You two know each other?" Martha asked curiously, her keen eyes assessing the situation.

"We've met," Ty said, a muscle along his lean jaw tightening.

"A long time ago-o-o," Lexi added as her body demanded another push.

Ty frowned and stepped to the end of the bed. "Unless I miss my guess, your protest is about to become a moot point. How long have you been having contractions, Alexis?"

When he tried to lift the sheet, Lexi planted her feet on the end of it. "My name is Lexi. And leave that sheet alone."

He pulled at the linen. She pressed her feet down more firmly.

"All right, Lexi. How long have you been in labor?"

"Since early this morning." She couldn't think of a more humiliating situation than her current position, and where Ty was about to look. They were really no more than casual acquaintances. "Get away from me."

He ignored her protest, freed the sheet and arranged it over her bent knees. "Why did you wait so long before you came to the clinic?"

"I didn't realize...I was in labor-r-r." Another wave of pain swept over her and she completely forgot her embarrassment as she rode the swell of the contraction. "I just...had a backache...until my water broke. That's when...the pain really became intense."

Ty's examination confirmed his earlier suspicions. Alexis was fully dilated and the fetus had entered the birth canal. "We'll have to put this argument on hold for a while, Lexi. You're about to have your baby."

Pushing his personal feelings aside, Ty's physician instincts took control. "We need to get her feet in the stirrups, Martha."

Martha nodded and moved the retractable equipment into place. "These new birthin' beds are the best thing to come along since penicillin. Maybe we'll get more maternity cases here at the clinic now that we have this little jewel."

"Where do most of the women go?" Ty asked as he tied his mask in place. "Granny Applegate?"

"Yep. Most of the women on the mountain have Granny come to their house." Martha chuckled at his disapproving frown. "Now, don't go gettin' your shorts in a bunch, Doc. She's a licensed midwife and when she runs into trouble, she always gives us a holler."

Ty didn't have time to respond to Martha's explanation when Alexis moaned and voluntarily lifted her feet to brace them in the stirrups. As he positioned himself at the end of the bed, his gaze locked with hers. Limp from perspiration, her golden brown hair had been pulled back with some type of clip, drawing his attention to the exhaustion marring her beautiful face. His chest tightened at the tears filling her emerald eyes, the trembling of her perfect lips, and the bright spots of color staining her creamy cheeks. She was extremely tired, in tremendous pain and understandably frightened. She needed the baby's father at her side, lending his strength, letting her know he was there for her when she needed him most.

"You're doing great, Lexi," he encouraged. "I can see the baby's head."

She nodded and squeezed her eyes shut. "It really hurts, Ty."

He felt her pain all the way to his soul. On impulse, he reached out, took her hand in his and gave it a gentle squeeze. "It won't be much longer. I promise."

The simple act of reassurance quickly had his insides churning with emotions he didn't have the time, nor the inclination, to sort through. Another contraction demanded their attention.

Supporting the baby's emerging head, he automatically urged, "I need you to give me one more big push and it will all be over."

As Alexis pushed with all her might, first one shoulder, then the other slipped free and the baby slid into Ty's waiting hands. Quickly suctioning the mucus and blood from the baby's mouth and nose, he watched the infant stare at him bleary-eyed for a moment, scrunch its little face, open its mouth and wail at the top of its tiny lungs.

The kid had the temper of a Chicago cab driver and enough volume to put a banshee to shame.

Ty smiled. "Martha, mark the time of birth," he said, clamping the umbilical cord in two places.

"It's a boy, Lexi!" Martha said happily, recording the numbers.

Alexis laughed. "Are you sure? I just knew I'd have a girl."

"Unless little girls have started comin' with extra plumbing, that's a boy," Martha said, chuckling. "What are you gonna name him?"

"Matthew."

Ty barely heard the two women as a crushing tightness filled his chest. No matter how many times he witnessed the miracle of birth, it never failed to fill him with a humbling sense of wonder, as well as a twinge of regret. Since he didn't intend to have children, he'd never have a moment like this to call his own.

Fred the Cream Puff was one hell of a lucky man. And the wimpy little jerk wasn't even here to realize it.

A mist clouding his eyes, Ty examined the squirming infant. Ten fingers. Ten toes. He grinned. An impressive sprinkler system.

But as Ty looked more closely at the baby, his smile faded and he felt the blood drain from his face. A tiny dimple dented the infant's chin, an inch of black hair covered his head and a small cowlick at his forehead caused his hair to part on one side.

Ty thought back to that night in Chicago. The one and only night he and Alexis had—

He stared in awe at the miracle he held, his gut clenching painfully as realization slammed into him with the force of a physical blow. The resemblance was more than just coincidental. It was undeniable. And that telltale little cowlick proved it. It had been a family trait for generations.

Tyler Braden had just delivered his own son.

Two

Ty handed Lexi her son, and while he dealt with the usual postpartum procedures, she focused her attention on the squirming infant in her arms. Matthew Hatfield's tiny fists flailed the air like a frustrated prizefighter, and his displeasure with the whole business of being born was written all over his little red face.

Love like she'd never known surged through her.

With a full head of black hair, a tiny dimple in his chin and a cowlick at the edge of his forehead, he was the most beautiful baby she'd ever seen—and the spitting image of his father.

The realization caused Lexi to glance up at the man who had unwittingly helped create the infant she held. How could fate be so cruel? Of all the hundreds of thousands of licensed physicians in the world, why did Tyler Braden have to be the one to take over the

Dixie Ridge Health Clinic while Doc Fletcher had his knee replacement surgery?

Ty was an experienced trauma specialist, for heaven's sake. One of the best in his field. Why wasn't he in some huge hospital, taking care of real emergencies? Why wasn't he seven hundred miles away—in Chicago—where he belonged?

A mixture of fear and apprehension filled Lexi to the depths of her soul as she watched Ty. Was he aware the miracle he'd participated in just happened to be the birth of his own son? And if he did realize the baby she held had been the result of their only night together, how would he react? Would he even care?

He hadn't said anything, but that did little to alleviate her fears. She didn't know him well enough to know how he'd react. He might be the type of man who could be a seething caldron of rage on the inside, yet appear to be the epitome of calm. She just didn't know.

When Ty reached over to lift the now sleeping infant and place him into Martha's outstretched arms, Lexi tensed. "Where are you taking my son?" She'd tried to keep her voice steady, but exhaustion and panic sharpened her tone.

"Don't worry, Lexi," Martha reassured. She hefted the baby onto her ample bosom and headed for the door. "I'm just gonna give this little man his first bath. Then, after Doc checks him over, I'll bring him in for you to nurse."

Lexi quietly watched Ty take her blood pressure and listen to her heart, when what she really wanted to do was jump out of bed, grab her son and put as much distance as possible between them and the clinic. Draping the stethoscope around his neck, Ty reached down to place his fingers on her wrist. Her skin tingled at the contact and her breathing became shallow.

Dear heavens, had she lost her mind? She'd just had a baby and her body felt as if she'd pushed a bowling ball through a keyhole. That should be enough to make her swear off men for life. The very last thing she should be feeling was any kind of awareness.

But whether she should or not, there was no denying its presence, or its cause. Ty had always had that effect on her. She could still remember the first time he'd spoken to her in the elevator of their apartment building. It had been the day he'd moved in. When he'd said, ''Hi. I'm your new neighbor,'' his smooth baritone had surrounded her like a soft velvet cape. And it had taken her a good fifteen minutes to get her pulse back down to normal.

After that they'd rarely seen each other. Until the night she'd lost her job and—

No. She wouldn't—couldn't—think about that now. If she did, panic would set in and she might give away her secret. At the moment, she was at his mercy and there wasn't any way she could get away from him.

''When will the baby and I be able to go home?'' she asked cautiously.

Ty ignored her question as he fought the turmoil raging within. He gritted his teeth and tried to ignore the feel of her soft skin beneath his fingers, the heated current traveling the length of his arm and exploding in his gut. How could he feel anything but contempt for Alexis after what she'd done? The shock of finding that he was the father of her child had damn near brought him to his knees only minutes ago.

"Everything appears to be fine with you and the baby," he finally managed to say. "Looks like the two of you will be going home in a couple of days." He hurriedly scribbled notations on her chart, snapped it shut and headed for the door. He had to get away from her before his cool facade cracked and his tangled emotions spilled out with the force of a raging river. "I'll be in to check on you later."

Knees that threatened to buckle carried him from the room, down the hall and into his office. Closing the door behind him, Ty leaned heavily against it.

He wanted answers and he wanted them now, but reason won out. Alexis needed to rest, and an upsetting confrontation at this point would be counterproductive. Besides, he wasn't sure he could talk to her without a serious breach of his professionalism.

A light tap on the door signaled that Martha had finished bathing the baby.

"He's ready for your examination, Doc," Martha called from the other side. "We'll be in exam room one."

Ty tossed the chart on the desk, then sank down in the chair behind it. "Bring him in here, Martha."

"While you get acquainted with our newest patient, I'm gonna run over to the Blue Bird Cafe and tell Freddie that everything went just fine," Martha said as she entered the room and handed Ty the precious bundle she carried. She paused for a moment, watching him cradle the infant to his chest. "I know this sounds like I ain't got the brains God gave a squirrel, but that baby sorta looks like you."

Ty couldn't have responded if his life depended on

it. When Martha quietly closed the door behind her as she left, he barely noticed. A lump the size of his fist clogged his throat, and the moisture suddenly misting his eyes was dangerously close to spilling down his cheeks. When the baby wrapped tiny fingers around one of his own, the lump in Ty's throat felt as if it grew to the size of a basketball.

Love, so fierce it was almost debilitating, raced through him as he stared down at his son. Ty had never allowed himself to believe a moment like this would be his to treasure. Never let himself entertain the thought of having a child of his own.

But no matter what reasons Alexis had for keeping her pregnancy a secret, Tyler Braden did have a son. And he'd be damned before he sat idly by and watched another man take his place in raising the boy.

For all he cared, the very squeamish, thoroughly inadequate Fred Hatfield could take a short leap off a tall cliff.

As long as it was in his power to prevent it, history would not repeat itself. Unlike Ty, Matthew was going to know his father and never feel the social inferiority that Ty had always felt.

He placed a kiss on the baby's forehead and made a solemn promise to himself and his son. "You're going to know I love you and that I'll always be there for you." He hugged the baby close. "And I'll walk through hell before I let Fred Hatfield or your mother stand in my way."

Lexi woke with a start, her heart pounding. She sat up and frantically searched the dimly lit room for the wicker bassinet Martha had placed Matthew in after he finished nursing.

It was nowhere in sight.

Panic tearing at her insides, Lexi reached for the call button, but her hands trembled so badly she couldn't engage the switch. Tossing it aside, she threw back the sheet and tried to get out of bed.

Her sore body protested the rapid movement and her knees threatened to give way when she stood, but she ignored the warnings. She had to find her baby.

By the time she crossed the room and made it down the long corridor to the deserted reception area, her flagging strength was all but spent and she had to lean against the wall for support.

"Martha—"

"Lexi, what in the name of all that's holy are you doin' out of bed?" Martha sent her swivel chair skating backward as she rose and hurried to Lexi's side. "I told you the first time you got up, I had to be there in case you needed help."

The room began a sickening swirl and Lexi felt herself start to sag. "Where's...my baby?"

"Doc, get out here," Martha yelled when Lexi leaned heavily against her. "Now!"

Just before Lexi lost her battle with the dark curtain closing around her, strong arms scooped her up and lifted her to a wide chest. Her nostrils filled with the essence of the man holding her. He smelled of spice cologne and...baby powder.

He must have been holding the baby when Martha called for help. The thought instantly cleared her fog-filled head.

Strength flowed from Ty's body to hers as he cradled her to him, and Lexi squeezed her eyes shut against the wave of emotion welling up inside her.

"Please, put me down."

"No."

"I can walk," she insisted.

"Yeah, right." Ty laughed, but the sound held little humor. "Trying to walk is what damned near had you kissing the floor."

Without another word, he carried her down the corridor to her room and tucked her into bed. At the loss of contact, Lexi suddenly felt cold and abandoned. It was a ridiculous feeling, considering the circumstances, but it was still very real.

With calm efficiency, Ty wrapped a blood pressure cuff around her upper arm, pumped air into it, then slowly released the valve as he listened with his stethoscope. Apparently satisfied with the reading, he took her pulse, recorded the numbers on her chart, then folded his arms across his chest to stare down at her.

"It isn't called labor for nothing, Alexis," he said, his voice stern. "Your body had to work very hard and use a lot of energy in order for you to give birth. And although I don't advise a patient staying in bed more than a few hours following a routine delivery, I do expect her to listen to orders."

Lexi ground her teeth to keep from screaming that it was his fault she'd gotten up, that she'd had a terrible nightmare in which he'd taken her baby. But caution forced her to remain silent. In no way did she want to arouse Ty's suspicions.

"As you recently found out, feeling faint is not uncommon the first time a woman tries to walk after giving birth," Ty continued to lecture. "That's why you were told to wait for Martha's assistance."

Lexi glared at him. "Are you quite finished, Dr. Braden?" When he gave her a slight nod, she asked the question foremost on her mind. "Where's my son?"

"He's right here," Martha said, wheeling the bassinet to the side of Lexi's bed. "He's been visitin' with Doc while you took a nap." Turning to Ty, she asked, "Are you sure you don't want me to stay?"

"Go ahead, Martha," Ty said, nodding. "I can handle things from here."

"Doc Fletcher always wanted me to be here when we had an overnight patient," she said, clearly miffed.

Ty shrugged. "Dr. Fletcher had a wife to go home to. I don't. Besides, I'll be here anyway. I have to get caught up on some paperwork and it'll take most of the night to get it done."

Hoping Martha proved to be as stubborn as always, Lexi's heart sank when she saw Martha hesitate. "Are you sure?"

"I promise I'll take good care of them," Ty said, smiling. "Now go home and get some rest."

Lexi watched with growing horror as Martha finally nodded and walked toward the door. "If you need me, you've got the number," Martha said, waving goodbye.

The very last thing Lexi wanted was to be left alone with Ty. In fact, she didn't want to be anywhere near him. The more time they spent together, the bigger the chance he'd realize he was Matthew's father.

As if to draw attention to that very fact, the baby let loose with a lusty cry.

"It appears somebody wants his dinner," Ty said. He picked the infant up, but seemed in no hurry to place him in Lexi's outstretched arms. "You said his name is Matthew?"

"Yes." Her apprehension intensified as Ty smiled fondly at the angry baby he continued to hold.

"Have you and Fred picked out a middle name?" he asked without looking at her.

Watching him stare down at the baby, Lexi frowned. "Did you meet Freddie this afternoon?"

"No." Ty chuckled when Matthew tried to find nourishment from the tip of his little finger. "I was with a patient. Maybe Fred and I will have the chance to get acquainted when he comes to take you and the baby home."

"Maybe," Lexi agreed.

All she had to do was keep the two from meeting. It shouldn't be hard, Lexi decided. She was quite confident that Freddie would be more than happy to wait outside the clinic.

"So, does this little guy have a middle name?" Ty asked again, interrupting Lexi's thoughts.

She searched his face, but his expression gave no indication of what he might be thinking. "Scott," she answered cautiously. "Why do you want to know?"

Ty finally handed the baby to her when Matthew found Ty's finger to be less than satisfying. "I need his full name for the birth certificate."

Relieved, Lexi managed a weak smile as she held her son close. "His name is Matthew Scott *Hatfield*."

"Of course," Ty agreed. Then, to her immense relief, he turned and left the room.

His son cradled to his chest, Ty sat in the darkened room, his eyes fixed on the sleeping woman in front of him. The months since she'd left Chicago had done nothing to lessen the effect she had on him. From the first time he'd laid eyes on her that day in the elevator, Alexis had taken his breath away with her beauty, had made his heart skip a beat when she spoke. She still did.

And earlier, when he'd carried her back to bed, the bittersweet memories of their night together had been overwhelming. The feel of her softness against him, the sweet smell of her honeysuckle-scented hair where it brushed his cheek, had made him feel as if he'd go up in flames.

But Alexis was off-limits now, married to another man. A man she was trying to pass off as Matthew's father. His jaw tightened involuntarily. Ty didn't think he'd ever forgive her for that.

He gazed down at the baby he held. Alexis may have replaced *him* with someone else, but Ty would never stand by and watch his son call another man "Daddy."

He smiled as his tension eased. He fully intended to let Alexis know he was aware of the truth.

And Ty knew exactly how to go about telling her.

Lexi's nerves were stretched to the breaking point. Time was slipping away. Fast.

If Freddie didn't show up soon to take her and the baby home, Ty would be back from his house calls. Her whole plan hinged on being gone before that happened.

When Martha walked into the room carrying an armload of fresh linens, Lexi tried to keep the anxiety from her voice as she asked, "Is Freddie out in the reception area?"

Setting the sheets on the bedside table, the older woman shook her head and began stripping the bed.

"Ain't seen hide nor hair of Freddie. And unless I miss my guess, we won't either."

Martha was right.

The smell of antiseptic and Freddie's delicate stomach were a dangerous combination. It would take a matter of life or death before Freddie Hatfield risked coming anywhere near the inside of the clinic.

Lexi walked over to the window on the far side of the room and parted the calico curtains. The sight of Freddie pacing uncertainly between the car and the clinic door made Lexi smile with relief. "I wonder how long Freddie's been out there."

Martha came over to peer out the window. "No tellin'." She laughed when Freddie stopped, glanced at the clinic door, then shook her head and started pacing again. "Goin' back and forth like that, Freddie's gonna wear a trench in the pavement."

As they watched Freddie's obvious dilemma, a shiny, red four-wheel-drive pulled into the parking lot. When the driver got out, pulled a black bag from the back seat and walked over to where Freddie stood looking helpless and forlorn, Lexi's blood turned as cold as ice.

Ty had returned and it appeared he was going to exchange polite conversation with her "husband," Freddie.

"Is something wrong?" Ty asked the obviously nervous woman.

"No," the blonde answered. A rosy glow tinged her cheeks when Ty's expression turned skeptical. "Well...sort of." She pointed a shaky finger at the clinic door. "I need to go in there...but I can't."

"Why not?" Ty asked, confused. "The clinic is open to everyone."

Her blush deepened as she struggled to explain. "It's...well, you see...I have this problem."

"What is it?" he gently coaxed. "I'm Dr. Braden. Maybe I can help."

"I don't think so," she said, her ponytail swaying from side to side as she vigorously shook her head. "I've tried to get over it. Really, I have." Her eyes pleaded for his understanding. "But there isn't anything I can do about it. It's a curse."

"What makes you think you're cursed?" Ty asked. He made a mental note to check the list of psychiatrists in Chattanooga. He just might be sending one of them a referral.

The woman closed her eyes, took a deep breath and blurted, "Aw, hell, Doc. The place makes me sick."

Ty wasn't sure what explanation he'd expected, but this wasn't it. "Excuse me?"

"It's the smell of antiseptic," she explained, clearly embarrassed. Her anxiety increasing, she twisted her hands into a tight knot. "Just one whiff of that stuff and I'll hurl in all directions."

Ty coughed to keep from laughing at her impassioned description. "I can see where that would present a problem," he agreed. "But I can't examine you out here in the parking lot."

"Oh, I'm not here to see you," the woman said hastily. "When I need a doctor, I go see Granny Applegate up on Piney Knob."

Ty frowned. Every time he heard the old woman's name or thought about her approach to medicine, he envisioned black cats and a steaming caldron of witch's brew. How could a young, seemingly intelligent woman place herself in the care of a quack like that?

"If you're not here to see me, then—"

"I'm here to take my sister-in-law and her new baby home," the woman interrupted. She gave the building a nervous glance. "But I can't let her know I'm here unless I go inside. And if I do that—"

"You'll get sick," Ty finished for her.

She seemed pleased he understood. "If you could just tell Lexi I'm here, I'd really appreciate it."

"Sure," Ty said, heading for the clinic entrance.

His disgust for Alexis's husband grew by leaps and bounds as he thought of the pretty blonde's dilemma. Evidently queasiness plagued the whole Hatfield family. Good old Fred had to have known the kind of anxiety his sister would suffer.

But did the man care how much hell he put the women in his life through? No. The ever-concerned Fred was a complete washout in the sensitivity department. How could any woman be attracted to a jerk like that?

Ty shook his head as he entered the clinic. There were some things about women he guessed he'd just never understand. He was beginning to think he didn't even want to.

Lexi turned away from the window, walked over to the bassinet and picked up the baby. In a few minutes Ty would be in to confront her with what he'd learned about her "husband." From there, it would be easy for him to figure out the rest of what she'd tried so hard to keep hidden.

She drew in a shuddering breath as she lowered

herself into the rocking chair and, holding Matthew close, set the chair in motion.

It wasn't that she wanted to keep Ty in the dark forever about his son. She'd never wanted that. But fear had kept her silent through the long months of her pregnancy, and now she needed time to come to grips with all that had happened. How was she supposed to tell a man who never intended to have a child that he'd fathered one?

"Lexi, do you feel all right?" Martha asked, concerned. "You look like you've seen a saint."

She wished what she'd just witnessed *had* been an apparition. At the moment, seeing a ghost sounded far more appealing than facing Ty.

"I'm fine," she answered, her voice far more calm than she felt. "I just want to take Matthew and go home."

"Can't say I blame you. Everybody rests better in their own bed." Martha finished tucking the corners of the sheet. "I'll get the birth certificate and a discharge paper for you to sign. Then you and that little angel can be on your way."

"I've taken care of it, Martha," Ty said, walking into the room.

Martha propped her hands on her ample hips. "If you keep doin' my job for me, we're gonna be havin' another long talk." Her menacing glare never wavered as she breezed past him.

"Great," Ty muttered, drawing Lexi's attention. "Another lecture."

Lexi's breath lodged in her throat at the sight of Ty, her fears and anxiety fading as she watched him cross the room.

Ty was, and probably always would be, the sexiest

man Lexi had ever seen. In a suit and tie he was sexy. But in jeans and a T-shirt, the man was downright sinful. The knit fabric, stretched across his wide shoulders and upper arms, drew attention to his well-formed chest muscles and bulging biceps. The royal blue color highlighted his deep, azure eyes.

The faded denim of his jeans hugged his long, muscular legs and emphasized his narrow hips. But from her seated position, it put certain other outlined areas on eye level as well.

Lexi swallowed hard when her pulse took off at an alarming rate. She had to have some kind of record-breaking hormonal imbalance. After the ordeal of giving birth not forty-eight hours ago, she shouldn't want a man within a hundred miles of her—and especially not Tyler Braden.

"I need you to sign this release form before you go," Ty said, handing her a paper and pen.

He reached down to take the baby and Lexi watched him cradle her son—their son—in the crook of his arm. Ty smiled when he put his index finger close to the baby's hand and Matthew wrapped his own tiny fingers around it. The sight was so poignant, Lexi had to look away.

Tears filled her eyes as she signed the release form Ty had given her. She wanted to tell him Matthew was his son, wanted Ty to be as happy about the baby as she was. But he'd told her once that he never wanted a child. And he'd been quite adamant about it.

When she'd asked him why he felt that way, his eyes had taken on a fierce gleam and he'd mumbled something about not being good with children. But watching him with Matthew now, Lexi knew for certain that wasn't the case.

"Your sister-in-law is waiting for you in the parking lot," Ty said.

Prepared to face the music, Lexi took a deep breath, rose from the rocking chair and handed him the paper. The moment of truth had arrived. She'd known a showdown with Ty was inevitable once he learned Freddie wasn't her husband. But she'd hoped for more time, hoped to put things in perspective before they discussed their son's birth and the bizarre circumstances of meeting again.

"Freddie has a real problem with the clinic—"

"I know," Ty interrupted, his disgust evident. "Doesn't he realize his sister suffers from a weak stomach, too?"

Shocked, Lexi barely managed to keep her mouth from dropping open. Evidently, Freddie hadn't introduced herself.

Lexi knew she was opting for the coward's way out, but at the moment, a hasty exit was far more appealing than a confrontation she wasn't prepared to deal with.

"I'm, uh, pretty sure Freddie knows the effect the clinic has on her." Lexi tried to keep her voice even as she reached for her son. "We'd better not keep your aunt waiting, Matthew."

When Ty continued to hold the baby, their eyes locked for a long, tense moment before he finally said, "You have to wait for a wheelchair."

"I don't need—"

"It's standard policy, Alexis."

"But that's ridiculous," Lexi protested. She waited for Ty to place Matthew in her arms, but when he just stood there glaring at her, she waved her hand to encompass the room. "Look around, Ty. You're in the Dixie Ridge Health Clinic. This place is a million miles away from the protocol that dictates a big city hospital. Besides, I'm perfectly capable of walking out of here."

"That may be, but for insurance purposes we have to follow procedure," he argued.

Martha wheeled the chair into the room, her expression revealing how she felt on the subject. "For what it's worth, Lexi, I think it's pretty silly myself." She gave Ty a withering glare. "Doc Fletcher never got bent out of shape when I let a patient walk out of here on their own steam."

"I'm not Dr. Fletcher," Ty stated flatly. He turned back to Lexi. "Now, if you'll have a seat, I'll take you and Matthew out to the car."

Desperation clawed at Lexi's insides. She didn't want to run the risk of Ty talking to Freddie again. With each meeting, the odds increased that he'd learn the truth. And although she fully intended to tell him everything, she didn't want or need the added complication of explaining in front of her sister-in-law.

"Alexis?"

"I told you my name is Lexi."

"All right, *Lexi*," Ty said, emphasizing her name. "Sit down."

Lexi glared at him. "And if I refuse?"

A gleam of determination lit his dark blue eyes. "I'll pick you up and carry you out."

"You wouldn't."

"Try me." His smooth baritone carried just enough edge to it that Lexi had no doubt he meant exactly what he said.

Several tense seconds stretched between them before she reluctantly gave in and lowered herself into the chair. "Now are you satisfied?"

He placed the baby in her waiting arms and didn't even try to hide his smug smile. She felt like punching him.

When Ty moved to take hold of the rubber grips on the back of the chair, Martha shook her head. "I'll take care of getting Lexi and the baby out to the car, Doc. It's *my* job. You're needed in exam room two, anyway. A thump rod on one of Carl Morgan's barrels popped loose and he's gonna need a couple of stitches to close a cut on his hand."

Ty looked bewildered. "Thump rod?"

Martha winked and Lexi smiled in spite of herself. "You can tell he's a city boy, can't you, Martha?"

Laughing, Martha nodded. "Stands out like Harv Jenkins's big toe when his gout's actin' up."

"You still haven't answered my question," Ty said stubbornly.

Relieved Ty wouldn't be taking her and the baby out to Freddie's car, Lexi managed to grin. "A thump rod is a part on Carl's…boiler."

"It's a technical term used by people in Carl's line of work," Martha added, her eyes twinkling merrily.

Ty frowned. "What line of work is Carl in?"

Lexi glanced at Martha, but the woman just shrugged. How much should they tell Ty? After all, he wasn't from the mountains and he certainly wasn't accustomed to mountain ways.

"He raises pigs," she said, finally settling on a half-truth.

"Then why would he need a boiler?"

"He uses it to cook up pig feed, Doc," Martha

answered. Her air of innocence almost made Lexi laugh out loud.

When Ty didn't make a motion to leave, Lexi asked, "Was there something else?"

He suddenly flashed a smile that sent a warm, fluttery feeling all the way to the pit of her stomach, then handed her an oversize envelope. "Here's Matthew's birth certificate."

The warmth remained with her all the way out to the base of Piney Knob Mountain. Freddie turned the car off the main highway and announced, "Mary Ann Simmons was right. That doctor is a real hunk."

"I suppose," Lexi said, trying to sound completely indifferent. Her attempt failed, but fortunately Freddie didn't seem to notice.

"He's real understandin', too." Freddie glanced in the rearview mirror at Lexi, where she sat next to the baby's car seat. "He didn't even bat an eye when I told him how I couldn't go inside the clinic because of the place makin' me sick."

"That's nice," Lexi said absently. Listening to Freddie extol Ty's many virtues was the last thing she wanted or needed to hear. To distract herself from her sister-in-law's chatter, Lexi removed the decorative parchment from the large envelope Ty had given her earlier.

Scanning the document, she felt her heart lurch to a stop, then take off at an erratic gallop. It wasn't the official birth record. That would be filed at the county clerk's office. But the complimentary certificate did reflect Ty's intentions.

And they couldn't have been more clear.

Matthew's surname had been recorded as Braden. And Ty had listed himself as the baby's father.

Three

Fall had always been Lexi's favorite time of year, but as she stared out of the car window, she saw none of the fall colors painting the mountain. One question kept swirling through her mind, screaming for an answer, blinding her with its implications.

What did Ty intend to do next?

By listing himself as Matthew's father on the birth certificate, he'd let her know—in no uncertain terms—he had something in mind. But what?

He thought she was married. Didn't he care about the problems his actions could cause if she really did have a husband?

"Lexi, are you all right?" Freddie asked when she opened the car door and peered into the back seat. "You look like you stuck your finger in a light socket."

Dazed, Lexi looked around. They'd driven up the

narrow, winding road to her cabin and parked without her even noticing.

The leaves on the maple and oak trees continued their daily transformation from green to shades of rust and gold. The marigolds she'd planted at the beginning of summer still bloomed heartily despite the crispness of the early fall nights. Birds still sang with the sweet purity of freedom. The chipmunk living under her front porch still scurried about, gathering acorns for the upcoming winter.

When so much in her life had changed, how could everything look just as it had only two days before?

"Oh, Freddie, nothing is ever going to be the same," Lexi said helplessly.

"Of course it won't," Freddie agreed. She unbuckled the seat belt holding the baby's car seat and lifted it from the back seat. "But don't worry. I'm sure every first-time mother feels a little overwhelmed at the thought of taking care of her baby."

Lexi glanced down at the birth certificate she still held. "I wish that was my only worry."

"You know Jeff and I will help." When Lexi made no move to get out of the car, Freddie gave her an exasperated look. "What's gotten into you, Lexi? You couldn't wait to get away from the clinic. Now you act like you don't want to go inside the house."

Sliding the parchment back into the envelope, Lexi slowly got out of the car. She'd fully prepared herself to shoulder the responsibility of being a single mother, had completely accepted how things had to be.

But the rules of the game had changed radically with Ty's unexpected reappearance in her life. By listing himself as the baby's father, did he expect to help her raise their son? Would he try to obtain custody of Matthew?

The thought sent a chill all the way to her soul. She needed someone to confide in. Someone who would listen and at least try to understand.

Lexi stared at Freddie for several seconds as Grandma Hatfield's sage words whispered through her mind. "A burden is sometimes easier to carry if you share it with someone you trust."

She had a burden, all right, and it weighed a ton.

Taking the handle of the baby carrier in her right hand, she hooked her left arm through Freddie's. When she spoke, her voice sounded surprisingly steady, considering her insides quivered like a bowl of gelatin in an off-the-scale earthquake. "Let's go inside, Freddie. There's something I need to tell you."

It wasn't as difficult as Lexi had thought it would be, and by the time they walked into the living room, Freddie was gaping at her.

"He's what?"

"You heard me," Lexi said calmly. "Tyler Braden is Matthew's father."

Freddie collapsed on the couch, her eyes wide. "But when did you two—I mean, where—"

Lexi placed the baby in the antique cradle that had held four generations of Hatfield infants. "When? Nine months, two weeks, and four days ago. Where? Chicago." She turned to give her sister-in-law a sardonic smile. "And before you ask how—the usual way."

Her sister-in-law shook her head as if to clear it. "You mean to tell me he's a doctor and he didn't recognize the symptoms of pregnancy?"

"We…" Lexi hesitated. No matter how she said it, it was going to sound bad. "We only spent one night together." She tiredly lowered herself into the rocking chair beside the cradle. She felt as if the weight of the world rested squarely on her shoulders. "It was the night before I left to come back home."

"But what about birth control?" Freddie asked. "I mean, him bein' a doctor and all, you'd think—"

"We did use something," Lexi interrupted. She shrugged helplessly. "But there isn't any method that's one hundred percent effective."

"Except abstinence," Freddie corrected. "And if you'd picked that method—"

"We wouldn't be having this conversation," Lexi finished.

Freddie rose from the couch and began to pace the length of the room. "Does he realize Matthew is his?"

"Yes."

When Freddie whirled around, her long, blonde ponytail slapped the side of her face. "I thought you told me he didn't know about the pregnancy." Her eyes narrowed and she propped her fists on her hips. "That woodpecker knew and waited all this time—"

"No," Lexi interrupted. "I haven't said anything to Ty."

"Then, how are you sure he knows?"

Lexi handed Freddie the birth certificate. "He must have figured it out, because he listed himself as the baby's father and Matthew's last name as Braden."

Freddie scanned the document, an incredulous expression crossing her delicate features. "Granny's garters! What do you think he'll do now?"

"I wish I knew." Lexi closed her eyes and rested

her head against the high back of the rocking chair. "But that's not all."

"There's more?" Freddie looked at Lexi as if she'd sprouted horns and a tail.

Lexi nodded. Any other time, they'd find humor in Ty's assumption about her marital status. But at the moment, Lexi couldn't find anything even remotely funny about the situation.

When Lexi remained silent, Freddie frowned. "I'm not going to like this, am I?"

"Probably not." Lexi grimaced as she struggled for the courage to meet Freddie's suspicious gaze. "He thinks I'm married to *you*."

Freddie looked as if she'd been pinched. "Grandpa's long johns! Where did he get a goofy idea like that?"

"Ty heard Martha and me talking about you," Lexi explained. "I guess he assumed by the name that 'Freddie' was a man and my husband."

"And you didn't set him straight." It was more an accusation than a question.

Lexi shook her head and stared down at her tightly laced fingers. "No."

Clearly confused, Freddie plopped back down on the couch. "Why not?"

Biting her lower lip, Lexi tried to keep a sob from escaping. When she finally gained control of her emotions, her voice quavered. "I guess I was trying to buy some time…until I could figure out what to do." Tears filled her eyes as she met her sister-in-law's disbelieving gaze. "Oh, Freddie, how could I have made such a mess of things? And why couldn't he have stayed in Chicago where he belongs?"

Freddie left the couch, knelt beside the rocking

chair and put her arms around Lexi. "Do you love him?" she asked gently.

"To tell the truth, I'd have to say I don't even know him," Lexi sobbed.

"Oh, holy cow! This just gets more and more bizarre every time you open your mouth."

Tears spilled down Lexi's cheeks, and she tried to swipe them away with the back of her hand. "Ty and I were neighbors. He lived down the hall and we rarely ever saw each other. We'd pass in the hall and speak, or say 'hello' as we got on or off the elevator. But that was it. Until…the night I quit the radio station."

"What made that night different?" Freddie asked.

Lexi took a deep breath. She'd started explaining things. She might as well finish. Besides, keeping secrets was precisely what got her into this mess to begin with.

"After a meeting with the corporate wonder boy in charge of restructuring the radio station, I decided there was no way I'd move my show to L.A. I didn't want to move that far from home, so I turned in my resignation—effective immediately—and cleared out my office. Everything I'd worked to build in the last five years had just disintegrated in less than thirty minutes, and I doubt I could have felt any lower." She sniffed back a sob. "When I went back to my apartment to pack, Ty had just gotten off duty at the hospital. He looked even worse than I felt."

Freddie nodded. "But how did you two get together?"

"He said he'd had a really bad day in the E.R. and I told him about losing my job." Lexi gave her sister-in-law a watery smile. "Ty suggested that we share dinner and a bottle of wine, since we'd both had a rotten day. I should have refused, but I didn't feel like being alone. So I accepted.''

''Who ended up where? Was the deed done at your place or his?''

''Freddie!''

''Sorry, Lex, but this is just like a soap opera.''

Lexi shrugged. ''My apartment had a gas fireplace and we picnicked in front of the hearth. He brought two bottles of wine and I supplied the cheese. We talked about being disillusioned with life and I told him about the peace I'd always found in these mountains and how I intended to come back here. Somehow, one thing led to another, and before either of us knew what happened, we were gathering our clothes and saying an awkward goodbye.''

Sitting back on her heels, Freddie shook her head. ''Geez, when I have a bad day, I feel lucky if Jeff plays a Garth Brooks CD and pops a pizza in the microwave so I don't have to cook supper.''

They remained silent for several minutes as the gravity of the situation sank in.

''I wonder what he'll do now,'' Freddie finally said.

''I'd like it if he just left me and the baby alone.'' Lexi wiped at a tear as it slid down her cheek. ''Forty-eight hours ago all I had to worry about was having a baby. Then, in less than a split second, my whole world is turned inside out.''

Freddie nodded sympathetically. ''I can imagine it was a real shock to find out the daddy of your baby was gonna be the one to do the deliverin'.''

''You have no idea.'' Lexi hiccuped. ''There I was, ready to give birth, when Ty walked in. What was I going to say? Oh, by the way, you just happen to be the father of the baby you're about to deliver. A child—'' her voice caught ''—you never wanted.''

''Now hold it.'' Freddie's pixielike features mirrored her confusion. ''How do you know he never wanted kids?''

''He told me that night.'' Lexi closed her eyes to hold back the threatening tears. ''Ty didn't say why, but I'm sure it had something to do with what he sees every day in the E.R.''

Suddenly overwhelmed, Lexi finally gave into the wave of emotion she'd held back since seeing Ty again. She cried for the circumstances surrounding their son's birth and the uncertainty of what Ty intended next.

Freddie held her while she sobbed, then handed her a tissue once the tears finally subsided. ''Maybe you're wrong about him not wantin' a baby.''

''I don't think so,'' Lexi said, wiping her cheeks.

''Jeff is never gonna believe this.''

''No!'' Her voice desperate, Lexi pleaded, ''Please don't tell anyone. And especially not Jeff. At least not until I have a chance to work this out with Ty.''

Her sister-in-law's hazel eyes filled with understanding. ''That would probably be best. Knowin' your brother, he'd go after the man with his double-barrel shotgun—''

''And all hell would break loose,'' Lexi finished for her.

They sat in silence for a time before Freddie asked, ''What's he doin' in Dixie Ridge, anyway?''

Lexi shook her head. ''I wondered that myself.''

Freddie rose to her feet. ''When do you think he'll let you know what his intentions are?''

"I don't know." Lexi rubbed at the pounding in her temples. "But I don't think I'll have too long to wait. I think what he did with the birth certificate is proof enough that Ty isn't the type of man to bide his time once he's decided on a plan of action."

Ty started counting mailboxes when he spotted the old wagon wheel leaning against a rail fence. In the city, he'd used building numbers, street names and well-known landmarks to find his way around. But here in the mountains, addresses weren't always that easy. He found himself looking for stumps and wagon wheels, counting mailboxes and relying on a tremendous amount of luck to find where he needed to go.

He turned onto the steep lane past the sixth box, a self-deprecating smile curving the corners of his mouth. When Martha informed him that he'd have to make house calls in order to treat a few of his older, less mobile patients, he'd thought the practice inefficient and outdated.

He'd been wrong.

The more he drove the winding roads snaking their way up the side of Piney Knob, the more Ty appreciated the morning ritual, felt a little more tension drain away. For the first time in more years than he cared to count, he was taking life at a slower pace, paying attention to things he'd never had time to notice before. He was beginning to like the difference in the way it made him feel, too. He liked being able to gear down and lower his guard. Not only was he getting to know the people on Piney Knob, he was beginning to know himself.

Ty gazed out the windshield at the panoramic view. Making house calls gave him the chance to enjoy the earthy tones of autumn painting the mountains with their rich hues, to see the ancient peaks and valleys shrouded with the smoky mists the area had been named for. He found he liked the frosty bite of the morning air, the clean smell of pine, instead of the sulfuric smog of the city. And this morning the practice provided another bonus.

Glancing at the packages in the passenger seat, his smile widened. Every patient on this morning's list of house calls had heard about the baby and asked if he would mind taking their gifts to Lexi. In doing so, they'd inadvertently handed him the perfect excuse to check on his son.

"Not that I need one," he muttered.

As far as he was concerned, being Matthew's father was reason enough for him to stop by the Hatfield place any time he damn well pleased.

He steered the truck around a sharp bend in the road, pulled to a stop in front of a small rustic cabin and looked around.

The place was nothing like he'd thought it would be.

In Chicago, Alexis's apartment had been highly fashionable, ultra modern and very expensive. But Lexi's house was humble and unassuming. The place looked like it had been constructed of giant Lincoln logs and might possibly have a little shed out back with a crescent moon carved in the door.

Ty shook his head as he got out of the truck and walked around to the passenger side to retrieve the gifts. He was having a hard time assimilating the two completely different lifestyles of the same woman. How could Lexi Hatfield be so different from her alter ego, Alexis Madison?

He heard the screen door squeak a moment before Lexi asked, "What are you doing here, Ty?"

He finished gathering the packages from the front seat before turning to face her. She didn't look happy that he'd dropped by. But that didn't matter. He had a right to see his son.

His arms loaded with presents, he walked toward the wide porch. "Some of my patients asked if I'd deliver their baby gifts."

"You could have taken them back to the clinic and had Martha call me." He watched her protectively fold her arms beneath her breasts. "Freddie would have picked them up."

Ty ground his teeth at the mention of Fred the Fearless. "I was in the area." Unable to hide his contempt for the man, Ty finished, "Besides, we both know good old Fred wouldn't make it past the front door." He started up the steps. "By the way, is he at home this morning?"

"No."

"Good."

"Ty—"

Their gazes locked for several tense moments as Lexi blocked his way. The wariness in her beautiful green eyes, the protective way she folded her arms in front of her, quickly had compassion tugging at Ty's insides. Fear was an emotion he'd never wanted or expected to solicit from any woman.

"These gifts are getting heavy," he said gently. When he saw indecision cross her flawless features, he urged, "Let's go inside."

Lexi hesitated before she finally opened the door and allowed him to enter. "You can put those on the table," she said, pointing to the kitchen area of the great room. "I'll look at them later."

Ty placed the packages where she'd indicated, then turned to study the rest of the house. The rustic log walls, crocheted rag rugs scattered across the polished hardwood floor, and large stone fireplace created a warm, cozy atmosphere. As he stared at the flagstone hearth, memories of their night together swamped him. A cold winter evening spent in front of a crackling fire, the flames illuminating the fine sheen of perspiration coating his and Lexi's bodies as they made love.

He shook his head and frowned. Remembering that night was wasted time and energy. She was married. If she spent any time snuggled against a man in front of a fireplace these days, it certainly wouldn't be with Tyler Braden.

"It was nice of you to take the time to bring the gifts," Lexi said from behind him. "But I'm sure you need to get back to the clinic."

"Not really." Anger surged through him. She could try dismissing him all she wanted, but he'd walk through hell before he allowed her to eliminate his presence in Matthew's life. "I've finished my house calls for the day and I don't have any appointments scheduled until later this afternoon." Careful to keep his expression as congenial as possible, he turned to face her. "Besides, I think it's time we had a long talk, Alexis."

"I told you my name is Lexi."

Ty smiled coldly. "Ah, yes. Alexis is your city name, isn't it?"

"Ty, don't—"

She looked so vulnerable, so wounded, Ty had to

stuff his hands into his jeans pockets to keep from reaching for her. He reminded himself of what she'd done, how she'd tried to keep Matthew from him.

''Where's the baby?'' he asked, surprising even himself at the harsh tone of his voice.

As if on cue, a soft mewling sound began and quickly grew into an impatient cry.

He watched her glance nervously at the hall. ''I'm sure you can find your way out.''

When she turned and started down the hall, Ty followed. ''I'd like to see how my son is doing.''

He could tell by the stiffening of her slender shoulders, the balling of her fists at her sides, that his statement had touched a nerve.

Well, that was just too damned bad. Finding out she hadn't bothered to tell him about his child had tapped a few nerves of his own.

Lexi suddenly spun around to face him, her eyes snapping green fire. ''Why are you here, Ty?''

''I told you, I want to see my son.'' He glared back at her. If she thought she was going to keep him from seeing the only child he never expected to have, she had a lot to learn. ''What's the matter? Are you afraid old Freddy boy will get angry about my being here?''

''Freddie has nothing to do with this.''

''You got that right,'' he shot back. ''I'm glad to hear you admit it.''

''You're impossible.''

When she turned away from him to storm through a door at the end of the hall, Ty followed. Stopping just inside the room, he glanced at the big double bed, his mouth tightening into a flat line. He didn't want to think about another man sharing that bed with her, holding her close, loving her beneath the colorful patchwork quilt. He knew it was ridiculous, but it caused a primitive, territorial feeling to race through him.

He turned to watch Lexi pick up Matthew and cradle him to her. She kissed the top of the baby's head and murmured something soft and soothing, then shifted her attention back to Ty.

"You'll have to come back another time," she said. "Matthew wants to nurse."

Ty shrugged. "So, let him. It's not like I've never seen a woman breast-feed." Why he dropped the hard edge to his voice, he wasn't sure, but the next thing he knew his tone sounded suspiciously seductive when he added, "Besides, I've seen your breasts before."

Her cheeks colored a rosy pink. "Ty, please don't—"

"Please don't what? Don't remember how beautiful your body was that night? How perfect your breasts are?" He shook his head. "There are some things a man never forgets."

"You'd better try."

Ty stepped forward to free the top button of her loose cotton dress. "Not in this lifetime, honey."

He didn't have any idea what the hell had gotten into him, but he couldn't seem to stop himself from releasing the second and third buttons. His fingertips grazing her satiny skin beneath the soft calico made him swallow hard and caused his body to tighten. He brought his hand up to caress her cheek, to trace her lips with the pad of his thumb.

Why couldn't things have been different? Why hadn't she contacted him when she discovered she was pregnant?

Obviously hungry and impatient, Matthew suddenly let out a loud wail.

The baby's cry brought Ty back to his senses as effectively as a bucket of ice water. He immediately dropped his hand and took a step back.

What the hell had he been thinking? She belonged to another man. And that was one boundary Ty had never, nor would he ever, cross. Besides, she'd intended to cut him out of his son's life.

"He's going to mutiny if you don't feed him," Ty said, his voice harsh.

She hesitated. "You aren't going to stay."

Ty nodded. "I want to spend some time with my son."

She gave him a look that would have sent a lesser man packing. Ty stood his ground.

But as she walked the short distance to the rocking chair in the far corner of the room, the gentle sway of her hips caused the muscles to tighten along his jaw as he fought against the familiar stir of desire. Having a baby hadn't diminished her alluring figure or detracted from her sensuous beauty in any way. In fact, it added a softness Ty found absolutely fascinating.

If he had any sense, he'd get in his truck, drive back down the mountain and take a dip in the ice-cold river flowing through the middle of Dixie Ridge. Instead, he shoved his hands into his jeans pockets, leaned a shoulder against the tall post at the end of the bed and hoped his smile looked less forced than it felt.

With her silky golden brown hair loosely tied back, her soft cotton dress moving gently around her perfect calves and her bare feet padding across the hardwood floor, Lexi looked like the quintessential earth mother. When she seated herself, unfastened the cup of her bra and guided her breast to the baby's eager mouth, Ty felt as if his insides had been set afire.

The intimacy of watching her nurse their child was overwhelming. And he knew for certain he'd never witnessed a more beautiful or poignant sight.

It changed nothing. She'd intended to keep the existence of his child from him. He'd do well to remember she couldn't be trusted.

Lexi cursed her crazy hormones as she settled back in the big, antique chair. When Ty had reached out to unbutton her dress and his fingers brushed the slope of her overly sensitive breast, her knees had threatened to buckle and her pulse had started pounding like an out-of-control jackhammer.

She heard his sharp intake of breath, could feel his intense gaze as he watched their son take her nipple into his mouth. But she refused to look at Ty, refused to allow him a glimpse of the tears threatening to spill down her cheeks.

When she'd been pregnant, she'd dreamed of sharing a moment like this with a husband, longed for the closeness the simple act could create between a couple. But the reality of the current circumstances was more of a nightmare than any kind of romantic fantasy.

"Does Fred know I'm Matthew's father?" he asked.

"Yes. But I told you, Freddie—"

"Good," Ty interrupted. His tight smile caused Lexi to shiver. "Then he won't be too surprised when you tell him I'm demanding joint custody."

She'd known from the moment Ty walked into the birthing room over a week ago that this conversation was inevitable. But she hadn't wanted it to be like this. Not with her breast exposed and him looming over her like a wild animal ready to pounce.

Her nerves stretched to the breaking point, she jumped when the pager clipped to Ty's belt beeped. She watched him press a button on the side and read the transmission on the tiny screen.

"We'll have to talk about this later," Ty said, his expression grim. "I'm needed at the clinic."

"I'm sure you can find your way out," Lexi said, careful to keep her voice even.

Their gazes met for a long tense moment before Ty promised, "I'll be back."

"I know."

Relief flowed through her when Ty finally turned and walked down the hall. She listened as he crossed the great room and left the house. Only then did she release the breath she hadn't been aware she was holding.

When Matthew finished nursing, Lexi changed his diaper, then placed her sleeping son in the cradle for a nap. "If your daddy thinks he can come in here making all kinds of demands, he's in for a rude awakening," she whispered.

Her emotions a tangled mix of anger, fear and anticipation, Lexi went to the front door to stare at the lane Ty had driven down only minutes before. Within the next few days, he'd be back to settle things once and for all. He'd have a lot of questions and want just as many answers.

But before she told him why she'd kept the baby a secret, Lexi had a few questions of her own. And before she agreed to joint custody, he'd better have some very good answers.

Four

A week and a half later, Ty had just stepped onto Lexi's porch when he heard it. It wasn't loud, and if the door hadn't been partially ajar, he probably wouldn't have noticed it at all. But once a man heard that sound, it left a permanent impression. Nothing sent a chill racing up a man's spine faster than the sound of a woman's heartbroken sobs.

He'd never in his entire life entered a house uninvited, but he didn't give the matter a second thought when he threw open the door and rushed into the great room of Lexi's small cabin. The late-afternoon shadows forced him to stop as his eyes adjusted to the muted light. He cursed even that small delay as he frantically searched for her.

Fear like he'd never known coursed through him when he found her curled up on one end of the large couch, Matthew cradled close to her breast. As a physician, he knew all too well the complications that could develop in an infant's first few weeks of life.

He knelt down in front of her. "What is it, Lexi? Is Matthew all right?"

She nodded, but when she raised her eyes to look at him, sobs wracked her slender body and a fresh wave of tears began to course down her cheeks.

"Is everything all right?" he repeated.

Nodding, she handed him the baby, covered her face with her hands and cried harder.

Ty checked Matthew to be sure and found him sleeping peacefully.

"Why are you crying?" Ty asked, thoroughly perplexed.

"I…don't…know," Lexi wailed, her face still buried in her hands. "But…I…can't stop."

Ty's confusion quickly gave way to understanding and an overwhelming sense of relief. He had a good idea what the problem was and the reason for the uncontrollable weeping. Lexi had a case of the "baby blues."

"I'll be right back," he said, rising to his feet. He walked down the hall to Lexi's room, settled his sleeping son in the cradle beside the bed, then made a detour into the small adjoining bathroom for a damp cloth.

It wasn't at all uncommon for a woman to experience unexplainable bouts of crying for several weeks after having a baby. Sudden hormonal changes combined with the responsibility and stress of taking care of an infant often overwhelmed a first-time mother. It was something a woman had no control over.

Glancing at the image of himself in the mirror above the sink, he felt guilt stab at his gut.

Great timing, hotshot.

Lexi was still trying to find her way as a new mother. A week and a half ago, he'd shown up demanding joint custody, adding a tremendous amount of tension to an already stressful situation.

That was something *he* could have controlled.

When he returned to the great room, Ty seated himself on the couch beside her and gently pulled Lexi into his arms. He bathed her face with the washcloth, but the gesture only made the tears fall faster. He finally abandoned his efforts and simply held her while her tears ran their course.

His guilt increased with each sob, and it wouldn't have surprised him to learn his picture would be inserted next to the word *jerk* in all future editions of *Webster's Dictionary*. It had been inconsiderate and insensitive to show up demanding his rights only a few days after she'd given birth. As a doctor, he should have known better. But as a first-time father, he was discovering that emotions often overrode years of training and common sense.

And his emotions weren't the only thing he was having trouble controlling. At the moment, with Lexi's face pressed to his shoulder, her warm breath feathering across the pulse at the base of his throat, his own hormones were doing their best to overpower his good intentions.

He'd only taken her into his arms to offer comfort. But his body wanted to offer a whole lot more.

Ty gritted his teeth and tried to think of something to cool the heat building inside him. Anything.

An image of the river flowing through the middle

of Dixie Ridge came to mind. The creeks and streams that ran down the mountain, and eventually emptied into it, were fed by underground springs. The water was ice-cold.

Ty mentally stripped off his clothes and dived in.

It didn't work.

He tried to think of Lexi's husband.

Snuggling on the couch with another man's wife wasn't the smartest thing he'd ever done. What if Fred walked in and found her in Ty's arms?

No help there.

The thought of Fred trying to take Ty's place as Matthew's father added an element of anger to the fire building in his gut. Nothing would please Ty more than the opportunity of taking a punch at the elusive man's nose.

He realized Lexi's tears had subsided when she sniffed and tried to push out of his arms. He tightened his hold. "Feel better?"

She nodded. "I'm…sorry. I don't know why that happened."

"It's pretty common."

Ty rubbed his cheek against her honeysuckle-scented hair. God, he didn't think he'd ever smelled a more heavenly scent.

"Please tell me…it won't happen again," Lexi said, her voice reflecting her embarrassment.

When she spoke, her lips brushed the column of his throat. His lower body reminded him the last time he'd made love had been with the woman he held.

"Normally, the mood swings don't last more than a week or two."

He stroked the length of her back and tried to tell himself he was only offering consolation. But deep down Ty knew the real reason he continued to hold Lexi, knew exactly why he didn't want to let her go. It felt so damned good to have her back in his arms, to have her soft, warm body pressed to his. How many times since that winter night in the city had he wished they'd had more time together?

Lexi felt Ty's warmth surround her, and a sense of coming home lit within her soul. He placed a finger beneath her chin, tilted her head back and kissed away the moisture still clinging to her lashes. Her pulse kicked into overdrive. His lips skimmed her forehead with aching tenderness. Her toes curled.

"It tears me apart to see you cry," he said, his voice rough.

The sound of his rich baritone sent tingles of anticipation skipping over every nerve in her body.

Lexi slowly met Ty's gaze. The look of raw hunger in his dark blue eyes took her breath.

"Hey, Lex, whose truck is that parked in the driveway?" a male voice called from the porch.

The man entering the cabin came to a dead stop at the sight of the couple cuddling on the couch.

Lexi jumped at the intrusion and quickly moved out of Ty's arms. She'd forgotten all about Jeff stopping by to fix the kitchen faucet.

She stood to face her brother. "I didn't expect you this early."

"That's obvious," Jeff said tersely, scrutinizing her appearance. She knew there was absolutely no way he'd miss the heightened color of her cheeks, her mussed hair or her labored breathing.

Ty slowly rose from the couch to stand beside her. "The SUV belongs to me."

"And just who the hell are you?" Jeff demanded, his accusing glare narrowed on Ty.

"Tyler Braden."

"He's the new doctor down in Dixie Ridge," Lexi added.

"My wife mentioned how helpful you were when she was at the clinic," Jeff growled. "But she didn't say anything about how friendly you are." He pointed to the couch. "Do you cozy up to all your female patients that way?"

Lexi glanced from her brother to Ty. Both men were eyeing each other like a couple of prizefighters competing for a title belt.

Jeff she could understand. He'd always been the overly protective older brother. But Ty?

Then, like a bolt of lightning, it hit her. Ty thought Jeff was her fictitious husband, Fred.

Great! This was just what her frayed nerves needed. She'd wanted a calm, private conversation with Ty about the birth of their son. Now she faced an explosive confrontation with the added bonus of an audience.

She had to do something. Fast. Once Jeff learned that Ty was Matthew's father, her brother would start throwing punches first and ask questions later.

"Ty, would you please check on the baby?" When he acted as if he intended to stay rooted to the spot, Lexi added a heartfelt, "Please?"

He looked as if he wanted to protest, but finally nodded and walked down the hall. She could tell by his stiff back that he wasn't at all happy about it.

Lexi watched until Ty was safely out of earshot, then turned to Jeff. Careful to keep her voice low, she pleaded, "Could you please come back later?"

Jeff rolled up the sleeves of his plaid flannel shirt, then folded his arms across his wide chest. "There's no way in hell I'm leavin' you alone with that guy."

"Why not?"

"Doctor or not, any man who puts the moves on a woman less than three weeks after she's had a baby can't be up to any good."

Lexi groaned. She recognized that stubborn look on her brother's face. Hell would freeze over before Jeff left without an explanation.

But she had to try. "I promise to explain everything later."

"No."

She watched him flex the well-developed muscles in his forearms. To get Jeff to leave now would take nothing short of a full-fledged miracle complete with thunder, lightning and a booming voice from above.

Or a feisty little pixie with fire in her eyes.

"Where's Freddie?"

Clearly confused by the unexpected question, Jeff gave her a look that said he thought she might be a few bricks shy of a full load. "At home. Why?"

She didn't bother to enlighten him as she walked over to the phone and punched in the number. To her relief, her sister-in-law answered on the second ring.

"Freddie, get over here," Lexi blurted. "Now."

"What's wrong?"

"Ty dropped by for a visit."

Freddie gasped. "And Jeff showed up to fix the faucet."

"You got it."

"Granny's garters! Have they started throwin' punches yet?"

Lexi glanced over her shoulder at her brother's

dark frown. "No, but you know Jeff. If he finds out about you-know-what before I can explain..."

"Hang on. I'll be right there."

Lexi hung up the phone, cursing her crazy hormones and men in general. Tears blurred her vision, then streamed down her cheeks to drop silently from her chin. What a perfect time for another crying jag, she thought disgustedly as she turned to face her bewildered brother.

"I'm going to have to ask a favor of you, little man," Ty said, leaning over the cradle to change his son's diaper. "I need for you to be a good boy while I settle things with your mom and Fred. Think you can do that for me?"

Matthew gazed up at Ty, waved his fists, kicked his feet and noisily sucked at the pacifier in his mouth.

"Good." Ty fastened the last tape on the diaper, then rocked the cradle gently. In less than a minute the baby's eyes closed and his pacifier stopped bobbing. "I knew I could count on your help," Ty whispered to his now sleeping son.

By the time he walked back into the living room, Lexi was sobbing uncontrollably and her husband was standing over her, looking like he faced the hangman's noose with no hope of escape.

"What the hell's wrong with her?" he asked, sounding desperate. "One minute she looked like she was ready to tear my head off, then all of a sudden she opened her mouth and started bawlin' like a baby."

Ty rubbed the tension at the back of his neck. "Hormone imbalance."

The man's cheeks colored a bright red and his mouth formed an *O* as understanding dawned. "Sorta like that monthly PMS stuff?"

Ty shrugged. "I guess that's a fair comparison."

He looked miserable. "What can we do to make her stop? I'd rather climb a barbed wire fence buck naked than listen to a woman cry."

Ty's stomach clenched. It would have been easy to take great satisfaction in the guy's misery, had it not been for the obvious concern written all over his face. Any fool could see Fred loved Lexi with all his heart and her tears were tearing him apart.

"What on earth have you two done to this poor girl?"

At the sound of the angry feminine voice, Ty looked up to see the blonde he'd met at the clinic throw open the door and rush into the house.

"Nothin'," the big man said quickly. When she glared at him, he looked beseechingly at Ty. "Tell her."

Before Ty could add his reassurance, the petite blonde put her arms around Lexi and led her to the couch. Turning on the men, she pointed to the door. "Outside! Both of you. And I better not hear your voices raised above a whisper. Is that understood?"

When they hesitated, she treated them to a look that had both men heading for the door with no thought of arguing the point further.

Ty raised a brow and shot the guy a startled glance when he muttered a subdued, "Yes, sweetpea," as they both tried to shoulder through the door at the same time.

Once outside, Ty sized up the man seated next to him on the porch steps. Fred the Cream Puff didn't look anything like Ty had imagined. Instead of a wimpy little guy with a sickly look, the man was every bit as tall as Ty, outweighed him by at least twenty pounds and appeared to be as healthy as the proverbial horse.

Ty stared at the thick stand of pines surrounding the yard. A flash of bright blue drew his attention, but he found no pleasure in his first glimpse of a mountain bluebird. He couldn't feel much of anything, beyond a numbing sense of guilt.

He'd tried to tell himself Fred was a complete jerk with no redeeming qualities at all. But Ty had just witnessed how much the guy cared for Lexi, how her tears had damned near brought the big man to his knees.

"I learned a long time ago not to cross my wife when she's in a snit," the man said. He grinned sheepishly. "It could be hazardous to my health."

"Sometimes retreat is the better part of valor," Ty agreed.

"You better believe it." The man blew out a deep breath. "My better half may be tiny, but I'll be the first to admit, dynamite comes in small packages."

Lexi was slender, but at five foot seven she certainly couldn't be considered petite. "Who are you talking about?" Ty asked, frowning.

"My wife. She may look like an angel come to earth, but when she gets on a rampage she can send the devil runnin' for cover." He laughed. "We're lucky she didn't have the time to work up a full head of steam before she threw us out."

Ty's mouth dropped open. "You're married to the blonde?"

"For the past seven years," the man said proudly.

He glanced toward the door, his smile loving. "She's really somethin', ain't she?"

Ty looked more closely at the man beside him. Although his hair was more a dark blond than golden brown, there was no denying the resemblance. He wondered why he hadn't noticed it immediately.

"You're Lexi's brother."

The man nodded as he pumped Ty's hand. "I'm Jeff Hatfield."

"I thought you were Fred."

Shaking his head, Jeff laughed. "Nope. Freddie's my wife."

Ty couldn't have responded if his life depended on it.

"Well, actually, her name is Winifred Mae Stanton-Hatfield," Jeff explained. "But she hates it. And don't even think about callin' her Winnie or Freddie Mae. You'll be sportin' a shiner in two seconds flat." He laughed and shook his head. "If you know what's good for you, you'll call her Freddie, same as everybody else."

Ty's logical mind tried to assimilate what Jeff had just told him. "Lexi isn't married," he said incredulously.

Mottled spots of anger crept across Jeff's cheeks. "No. She came home near ten months ago, single and jobless. When we found out she was pregnant to boot, Freddie and I tried to get her to tell us who left her high and dry, but she flat out refused. I even told her I'd go after the bastard with my double barrel and see that he done right by her."

Ty stiffened at the all too familiar term, but recovered enough to ask, "What did she say to that?"

"She told me it was none of my business," Jeff

said, clearly exasperated. "Can you believe that? Some city slicker leads my only sister down the primrose path and I'm supposed to forget all about it."

Staring at his hands clasped loosely between his knees, Ty took a deep breath, then met Jeff's angry gaze head on. "She apparently felt the same way about the baby's father."

"What do you mean?"

"She didn't tell me either."

Jeff looked as if he'd been smacked between the eyes with a baseball bat. "You...you're the lowdown, no good—"

"Yes."

Jeff jumped to his feet, his hands balled into tight fists. "Oh, I get it. My sister was good enough to take to bed, but not good enough to walk down the aisle. What kind of man are you? How could you just stand back and let her go through all this by herself?"

Ty stood to face Jeff, his own fists ready. "I wouldn't have if I'd known—"

When the punch came, Ty was ready for it. Using a survival trick he'd learned in his teens, he moved swiftly to block the right cross, then twisted Jeff's arm behind his back and held it as he tried to reason with the man.

"I didn't know anything about the pregnancy. In fact, until the day I delivered the baby, I hadn't seen or heard from your sister since she left Chicago."

Jeff struggled to free himself, then turned to face Ty. The fight seemed to drain away as he recognized the truth in Ty's steady gaze.

"Damn! You really didn't have any idea she was pregnant, did you?"

"Not a clue."

"Lexi Gail Hatfield! Get out here."

Seconds later the door opened, but instead of Lexi, Freddie stepped out onto the porch. Planting her hands on her hips, she warned, "Jeff Hatfield, I thought I made it clear I didn't want to hear your voice raised."

"That sister of mine has a lot of explainin' to do," Jeff growled. He pointed to Ty. "Braden is the baby's daddy and she didn't even bother to tell him."

"I know," Freddie said calmly.

Caught off guard by his wife's admission, Jeff opened and closed his mouth several times before he could speak. "And you didn't tell me?"

Freddie smiled. "No."

Jeff folded his arms across his chest as he glared at his wife. "Why not?"

"Lexi made me promise." Freddie's eyes lit with mischief. "Besides, Love Dumplin', there are some things men just don't need to know."

The horror on Jeff's face at Freddie's use of the obviously private endearment had Ty clearing his throat to keep from laughing out loud. But when she blew Jeff a kiss as she went back inside, Ty couldn't keep from smiling.

"Love Dumpling?"

"You didn't hear that," Jeff warned.

Ty's grin widened. "Hear what?"

Jeff slumped down on the steps, his cheeks bright red. "Women!"

"There's no figuring them out," Ty commiserated. He sat beside Jeff and stared off into the distance. "I still can't understand why Lexi didn't get in touch with me as soon as she found out she was pregnant."

"That must have been a hell of a shock when she finally did tell you."

"She didn't," Ty said, his tone reflecting the betrayal he still felt. "I had to figure it out on my own."

"Then how do you know for sure the baby is yours?"

"There's no doubt about it. The timing is right and he looks just like me."

Jeff chuckled. "With all that red, wrinkled skin, how can you tell? To me, all babies look alike."

"He also has a cowlick just slightly left of the center of his forehead. Just like mine. It's a family trait."

They sat in silence for several minutes as Jeff digested what Ty had told him.

"Did Lexi finally fess up and tell you why she didn't say anything?" Jeff asked.

"No." Ty heaved a sigh. "But you can bet I intend to find out."

Lexi sat on the couch, dabbing at the last of her tears with a crumpled tissue. "What are they doing now, beating each other to a bloody pulp?"

From her vantage point at the window, Freddie gave a disgusted snort. "It looks like they're laughin'." She shook her head as she walked over and plopped down in the rocking chair. "If I didn't know better, I'd swear they were long lost buddies. But you know Jeff. He could be plannin' just about anything."

"Men," Lexi muttered.

"You can't live with 'em and you can't shoot 'em," Freddie agreed, heaving an exaggerated sigh.

Both women nodded in solemn agreement, then burst out laughing.

"Thanks," Lexi said. "I needed that."

"I figured you did." Freddie glanced at the door. "How long do you think it will be before Ty comes in here demandin' answers?"

Lexi shrugged. "I'd say just about any time. By now I'm sure Jeff has explained that you're Freddie and enlightened Ty about my marital status."

"Do you want me and Jeff to stick around in case you need moral support?" Freddie offered.

Tempted, Lexi finally shook her head. "It would be best if we worked this out on our own." She stood, straightened her shoulders, then started for the door. "He's not the only one with questions."

"Atta girl, Lex," Freddie said, grinning. "Take the bull by the horns."

Lexi winked. "Or the doctor by his stethoscope."

"Oooh, that sounds kinky." Her expression turning serious, Freddie rose to leave. "I hope you get the answers you want."

Her voice little more than a whisper, Lexi said, "Me, too."

"If you need us, all you have to do is pick up the phone. We can be here in less than five minutes." Freddie hugged Lexi close for several seconds, then opened the door to announce, "Jeff, it's time for us to go home."

Ty and Jeff stood to face the two women as they walked out of the house.

Jeff stubbornly placed his hands on his hips. "But Lexi and Braden—"

"Have things they need to talk over," Freddie stated. "And they don't need us to do it."

Jeff looked as if he wanted to protest, but his wife's don't-even-think-about-it frown stopped him short.

Turning, he extended his hand to Ty. "Good luck, Braden."

"Thanks." Ty shook Jeff's hand, then glanced at Lexi. The determination he saw sparkling in her dark green eyes had him adding, "I have a feeling I'm going to need it."

When her husband continued to linger, Freddie prompted, "Come on, Jeff. You've got work to do at home."

Jeff looked confused. "I do?"

Freddie nodded. "Granny Applegate said the moon is right for makin' a baby tonight, Love Dumplin'." She walked up to wrap her arms around his waist. "And I can't do it by myself, big guy."

Jeff gave Ty a wicked grin. "Aw, hell. It's a dirty job, but somebody's got to do it." Reaching out he grabbed Freddie's hand and hurried her along as he headed for the path leading down the mountain. "See y'all later."

Ty watched the couple disappear into the thick forest at the edge of the yard, before turning to face Lexi. She looked thoroughly exhausted.

"I suppose you'd like some answers," she said, motioning for him to follow her into the house.

"Are you sure you're up to this?" he asked, closing the door behind them.

"No. But I don't think waiting will make it any easier."

Ty walked over to where she stood. "You're probably right."

She looked tired, but so damned determined, he didn't think twice about taking her into his arms. He'd always admired strength and independence, found it incredibly sexy in a woman.

Pulling her close, he gazed down at her. "Do you have any idea what a relief it is to find out you aren't married?" he asked, his voice husky. "For the past few weeks, I've been on one hell of a guilt trip."

"Why?"

"Lusting after another man's wife has never been my style," Ty said. He lowered his head. "And because I've wanted to do this since I walked into the birthing room weeks ago."

Five

Ty crushed Lexi's lips beneath his, chastising her for the deception. But as his mouth moved across hers with bruising pressure, desire quickly erased his feelings of betrayal and he eased the kiss to trace her lips with his tongue.

She was soft, warm and, to his satisfaction, very receptive to his gentle probing. Teasing, encouraging her to allow him entry, he reacquainted himself with the sweetness he'd found the night they'd conceived Matthew.

He tightened his hold and fitted her more fully to him. The scent of honeysuckle and sunshine filled his nostrils. He didn't think he'd ever smelled anything quite so sexy. Her full breasts pressed to his chest, her softness melting against his hard contours, and her moan of desire made Ty's body grow tight with need.

His immediate and totally predictable response caused his jeans to feel as if they'd shrunk.

The discomfort helped to restore some of his sanity. He wanted her, had wanted her from the first day they'd met. But she couldn't make love this soon after giving birth. Besides, there were too many unresolved issues between them. Too many questions he deserved to have answered.

Summoning every ounce of strength he possessed, he broke the kiss. He forced himself to pull back and turn away to keep from reaching for her again.

"Before this goes any further, we'd better talk," he said, his voice less than steady.

Lexi's knees felt like the tendons had been replaced with stretched out rubber bands as she walked over to the rocking chair. If she didn't sit down, and soon, she knew for certain she'd collapse in a heap on the floor.

Ty's kisses had been potent that night in her apartment. But today they had gone way beyond powerful. Today they had been downright debilitating.

The moment his lips touched hers, she'd forgotten all about the problems they faced now, or how they would resolve them. He'd taken all that from her and left her with nothing but the ability to feel.

Lowering herself into the chair, she watched him settle himself on the couch. He leaned his head back against the soft leather, obviously struggling with what he wanted to know first.

She knew this had to be very hard for him. But then, she found it no less difficult.

"It's not like I got pregnant on purpose, Ty," she stated, deciding to get things started.

He shook his head. "I never thought you did."

"I didn't find out until several weeks after I returned home."

"I figured as much." He sat forward, the only outward sign of his emotions reflected in the tightening of his jaw. "But it doesn't explain why you failed to tell me about the pregnancy. Didn't you think I had the right to know?"

"I wanted to tell you."

"Then why didn't you?" He shot up from the couch and began to pace. "Didn't it occur to you that I might want to have a say in the choices you made?"

Lexi took a deep breath. "I knew exactly how I wanted to handle the situation."

He whirled around to face her. "And my input wasn't needed?"

"I didn't say that."

He stopped in front of her, the color on his lean cheeks heightened by his anger. "What *are* you saying?"

Lexi sighed. "I wanted my baby, Ty."

"*Our* baby. He's my child, too."

"Yes."

She'd known their discussion would be arduous at best, but she still hated having to vocalize what she'd feared all those months ago. Folding her hands in her lap to keep them from trembling, she steadily met his furious gaze. "I thought you might try to convince me to terminate the pregnancy."

He sucked in a sharp breath. "What made you think I'd want that?"

"What else was I to think?" she asked. "You made it perfectly clear that night that you never intended to father a child."

Ty felt his anger drain away as his words came

back to haunt him. He had felt that way. He still would, if he hadn't known about Matthew. But Ty did know. And that changed everything.

He rubbed the tension building at the base of his neck. "Circumstances are different now."

Lexi stood to face him. "Because you know about the baby?"

"Yes."

"Why didn't you want a child, Ty?" She placed her hand on his arm. "I've seen you with Matthew, and I can tell you like children."

He ignored her question. He wasn't ready to share his reasons, to watch the disgust fill her emerald gaze. "Whether I ever intended to or not, I did father a child. And I'm going to take responsibility for him." Ty met her questioning look. "You deprived me of the knowledge I was going to be a father, but you won't keep me from being a major part of his life, Lexi."

"What makes you think I'd want to do that?" she asked, looking shocked.

"Because you've had ample opportunity to set the record straight." Unable to keep a hard edge from his voice, he continued, "But you didn't. And if I hadn't put everything together, you would have let me continue to believe that Matthew belonged to another man."

Obviously startled by his impassioned statement, she gasped. "No."

He placed his hands on her shoulders as he gazed down at her. "Why did you lie to me, Lexi?"

"I didn't lie," she insisted, her slender body trembling beneath his hands.

Ty ground his back teeth as he struggled for control. Losing his temper wouldn't accomplish anything. "No, but your omission of the facts was the same as if you had lied. You knew I thought you were married. And not once did you try to set the record straight. Hell, I didn't even know your real name. I thought you were Alexis Madison."

"That was my on-air name. The radio station thought Lexi Hatfield sounded too country."

"So Alexis Madison was born," Ty guessed. He knew it was unreasonable to expect more of her than he was willing to give himself. But at the moment he wasn't feeling very rational. "You were ashamed of your background?"

"No." She glared at him. "I'm not the least bit embarrassed that my father was a carpenter with an eighth-grade education. Or that my mother went straight from high school graduation to changing diapers. I come from good, honest people and I'm proud of them."

"How did they feel about the concessions you made for your career?"

"They were killed in a car accident when I was fifteen," she said sadly. She paused a moment before she gave him a defiant look. "But had they lived, I'm confident they'd have understood and supported my decision to go along with the name change. Just as I'm sure your parents supported your decision to become a doctor."

Lexi watched Ty stiffen at the mention of his family, watched him shutter his emotions as effectively as if he'd lowered a curtain.

Anger, swift and hot, swept through her. She placed her fists on her hips. "Oh, so that's the way it is, huh? We can dissect my family. We can question my decisions and motivations. But yours are off limits.''

His expression indicated that she was correct in her assessment of the situation. ''Why should my background matter?'' he asked defensively.

''It's part of my son's—''

''Our son.''

''*Our* son's heritage. He'll want to know your family, want to know how their influence made you the man you are.''

His stony silence and guarded expression spoke volumes. If she hadn't realized it before, she did now. Ty wanted to be part of Matthew's life, but not hers.

''Can you at least explain what you're doing here?'' she asked.

''I wanted to see my son.''

Lexi shook her head. ''No. I mean why did you come to Tennessee? You're one of the top trauma specialists in Chicago, Ty. Why did you take over something as tame as the Dixie Ridge Health Clinic?''

''It's only temporary. I'll be going back to the city in a few months.''

''I know. But why did you leave Chicago in the first place?''

''Does it matter?''

He was hiding something. She was sure of it. Was his reluctance to talk about his past or his present plans a way to keep her from finding out that he intended to take her son with him when he left Dixie Ridge? Where they might go if he did?

Feeling a chill spread throughout her soul, Lexi took a deep, steadying breath. ''I see no reason to carry this any further. You seem to feel my life should be an open book, but yours is off-limits. But it doesn't work that way.'' She walked to the door. ''I think it would be best if you leave, Ty.''

He looked as if he wanted to argue the point, but when she opened the door and stood beside it, he walked out onto the porch. ''I'll come back another time to finish our discussion about joint custody.''

As he descended the steps, Lexi advised, ''From now on, when you want to see Matthew, I'd appreciate if you'd call before you drop by.''

After finishing his morning house calls, Ty drove down Piney Knob. He paid little attention to the picture-postcard scenery or the crisp smell of autumn on the October breeze. He wasn't even able to manage more than a curious glance when he passed Carl Morgan on his way up the mountain, the man's truck piled high with bulging burlap bags and crates of plastic gallon jugs. For the past week, Ty had been desensitized to anything except the heavy feeling of regret that followed his conversation with Lexi.

Her accusations about his reserve had been right on the mark. He did keep certain aspects of his life locked deep inside. But it was more a measure of damage control than anything else. He'd learned long ago that if he didn't want to hear the inevitable condemnation that would surely accompany his revelation, silence was his best defense. He'd only revealed his secret to one woman in his life—a woman he'd thought cared deeply for him—and he'd never forget the sting of rejection that had followed.

Steering the truck into the clinic parking lot, he got out and reached into the back seat for his medical bag. Some things were better buried, never to be ex-

humed. He wanted to keep it that way. He didn't want
to face the inevitable ridicule that would accompany
his confessions. Or, worse yet, the accusations. He
saw enough of those each night in his dreams.

Forcing the disturbing thoughts from his mind, he
pushed open the clinic door.

Martha glanced up from the book she'd been reading. "You look like somethin' the dog dragged up
and the cat wouldn't have. Haven't you been gettin'
enough sleep?"

"I'm fine, Martha."

He should have known the eagle-eyed nurse would
notice, and feel it her duty to comment on, his haggard appearance. Hoping to divert her inevitable questions, he asked, "What does it look like today? Do
we have many appointments?"

"Nope." Martha checked the few folders in the
wall pocket beside the desk. "Looks like the rest of
the mornin' is free and clear. Your first patient isn't
scheduled until afternoon."

Ty nodded and walked past her. "If you need me
for anything, I'll be in my office." When the ample
nurse followed him into the small room at the back
of the clinic, he frowned. "Was there something else,
Martha?"

He almost groaned aloud when Martha patted the
thick roll of gray hair at the base of her neck and
straightened her pristine smock. He didn't feel up to
another lecture. But whether he wanted to hear it or
not, once she started the ritual, Martha was impossible
to stop.

He shrugged out of his jacket. "What have I done
this time, Martha?"

"I like you, Doc." She eyed him over the top of

her glasses. "You've still got a ways to go, mind you. But for a city boy, you're showin' a lot of promise."

"Thank you, Martha," Ty said, surprised. He could have sworn the woman thought him a total incompetent. "Coming from you, I consider that quite a compliment."

"That's why I'm gonna have my say," she stated, her look defying protest.

Apprehension plucked at the hairs on the back of Ty's neck as he hung his blazer on the coat tree, then moved to the chair behind his desk. He had the distinct sensation of waiting for the other shoe to drop. Knowing Martha, he didn't figure he'd have long to wait.

He didn't.

"Just how much time are you gonna waste before you do right by Lexi Hatfield?" she asked, placing her hands on her wide hips.

Ty was grateful he'd been in the process of seating himself. Otherwise, he might have landed on the floor. If he thought he'd been surprised by Martha's backhanded compliment, it was nothing compared to the shock racing through him at that very moment. How had she discovered the truth?

At his obviously dumbfounded expression, Martha nodded. "That's right. I know you're that baby's daddy. Now what are you gonna do about it?"

Ty cleared his throat and tried to regain both his voice and composure. "Who—"

"Nobody had to tell me," Martha interrupted. She tapped her glasses with a wrinkled finger. "I may have to wear bifocals, but I ain't blind. That fuss Lexi kicked up when she found out you'd taken over the clinic was enough to raise my antennae. Then you admitted the two of you had met before." She shrugged. "It didn't take a genius to figure out the rest. Besides, any fool can see that child looks more like you every day."

Ty felt as if the breath had been knocked out of him. "How long have you known?"

"About as long as you." Martha gave him a sympathetic smile.

"But you haven't said anything." He rubbed at the tension creasing his forehead. "That's not like you, Martha."

She settled herself in the chair across the desk from him. "I figured you and Lexi would get things straightened out, go see Preacher Green and everything would be put to rights. But for the past week you've moped around like a bloodhound that's lost his nose." Her keen eyes assessed him once again. "What happened? Did she turn you down?"

Ty winced. Martha wasn't going to like his answer. "I didn't ask."

"And why not?" Compassionate before, Martha's eyes had turned to glittering chips of blue ice.

"It's complicated."

Martha snorted. "Only because the two of you make it that way. Did you love her?"

Ty stared at the crusty nurse. Hell, he didn't even really know Lexi. Oh, he'd liked her immediately when they first met in the elevator of their apartment building two years ago. And he'd wanted her almost just as long. But love?

"Well, did you?" Martha persisted.

Discussing his acquaintance with Lexi wasn't going to be easy without making it sound exactly like what it had been—a one-night stand. "No, I can't honestly say that I loved Lexi. I liked her. A lot.'' He chose his next words carefully. ''But she left to come back here and we didn't have a chance to explore anything further.''

Martha looked grim. ''Well, I've known lots of folks that started out with less. I guess you can learn to love each other after the deed's done.''

''What are you talking about, Martha?'' Ty wasn't at all comfortable with the direction Martha was taking the conversation.

''I'm talkin' about the two of you doin' the right thing.'' She folded her arms beneath her ample bosom. ''When are you gonna marry her?''

Ty stared at the older woman for several seconds. An image of Lexi in his arms as he made love to her every night for the rest of their lives, holding her while she cried out his name, flashed through his mind. Blood surged to the lower region of his body, making him light-headed.

He gulped hard and shook his head to clear his wayward thoughts. ''Have you lost your mind, Martha? I just told you that we liked each other, but we aren't in love.''

''I ain't deaf. I know what you said. But right is right. I've seen a lot of marriages based on a whole lot less than the couple likin' each other.''

''But—''

''No buts about it,'' Martha interrupted. ''I've known Lexi Hatfield all her life. You can bet your bottom dollar if she liked you enough to sleep with you, her feelings could run deeper, given the time. Now get the lead outta your shorts and pop the question.''

''I know what her answer would be if I did.'' Ty

shook his head. He couldn't believe he was actually giving the idea consideration.

"Think she'd say no, huh?"

"I don't *think*, Martha. I *know*."

"Then you need help."

Apprehension once again tingled across his scalp. "I don't think—"

Martha ignored him. "Does Jeff Hatfield know you're the baby's daddy?"

"Yes, but—"

"I'm surprised he hasn't already thought of it," she said, grinning.

Ty's hair felt as if it stood straight up. He had a feeling he knew what she had in mind. "Don't even think about it, Martha."

She laughed and treated him to a conspiratorial wink. "Ever heard of a shotgun weddin', Doc?"

"Freddie, I don't need a new dress," Lexi protested as they drove down Main Street. "I have more clothes now than I'll ever wear."

"Those are city clothes," her sister-in-law insisted. "Since you're not goin' back to Chicago, you need country duds."

Lexi pointed to her T-shirt and jeans. "In case you hadn't noticed, I'm wearing the same thing you are."

"But I don't have some designer's name plastered across my butt," Freddie shot back. She parked the car in front of Miss Eunice's Dress Shop. "Besides, you've been cooped up in the house with the baby for the last month and a half. You need to get out, even if it is just for a couple of hours."

"But I feel guilty about being away from Matthew."

"We both know Martha will take good care of him," Freddie said, clearly losing patience.

"She'll spoil him rotten," Lexi muttered.

"No more than I already have." Freddie got out of the car and came around to open the passenger door. "Now get your butt outta that seat so we can try on some clothes."

Lexi reluctantly left the car. She'd never seen Freddie so persistent. If she didn't know better, she'd swear her sister-in-law was up to something. But for the life of her, Lexi couldn't imagine what it would be.

Sighing, she opened the shop's door. It didn't matter. How much trouble could Freddie get her into in Miss Eunice's Dress Shop anyway?

Miss Eunice McMillan parted the curtain behind the counter to peer at the three men in her stockroom. "They just pulled up out front."

His grin wide, Jeff checked his watch, then winked at Ty. "Right on time."

Ty watched the elderly woman's head slip back through the curtain as the bell over the door tinkled merrily. His stomach did a backflip when he thought of what they were about to do. This had to be the craziest stunt he'd ever been involved in. And he still couldn't believe he'd gone along with it. But the more he'd thought about it, the more he'd warmed up to the idea. He'd not only get to be a full-time father, he'd share his life with the most alluring woman he'd ever known. That is, *if* he could convince her to return to Chicago with him. He didn't want to think about what would happen if she wouldn't.

He eyed the double-barrel shotgun Jeff held and

rubbed his hands against the legs of his trousers to
dry his sweaty palms. At one point, Ty had tried to
back out of the scheme, reasoning that it would be
better to go the more traditional route of courting
Lexi, then asking her to marry him. But his soon-to-
be brother-in-law wouldn't hear of it.

"Are you certain that gun isn't loaded?" Ty asked
for the tenth time since they'd taken their places in
the storeroom.

Jeff chuckled as he released the catch, broke the
gun down and revealed two empty chambers. "Don't
worry, Braden," he said, his voice hushed. "I
couldn't shoot you, even if I wanted to." He snapped
the gun back together, then held it out for Ty's in-
spection. "Both triggers are broke off. The only reason I keep it is because it belonged to my grand-
daddy." He narrowed his eyes. "But don't go gettin'
any ideas. I've got one at home that works just fine."

Unwilling to put Jeff to the test, Ty nodded and
turned his thoughts to more pressing matters. He
hoped the seams of the ill-fitting tuxedo jacket held
just a little while longer. Used for the shop's wedding
display, the damn thing had to be twenty years old
and two sizes too small.

For the past two weeks, Martha, Freddie and Miss
Eunice insisted everything was under control, that he
didn't have a thing to worry about. They'd made all
the arrangements, planned down to the very last detail
and selected everyone's clothes. Martha had even
pulled in a few favors down at the county courthouse
and made arrangements for the marriage license without Lexi having to be present to obtain it.

At the time, Ty had been more than happy to let
them handle things. The less he knew about the plan,

the less he had to deny. Now, standing in a tuxedo that threatened to burst at the seams across his shoulders and was way too tight in certain sensitive regions below his belt, he wished they'd at least consulted him about his size.

"What are they doing now?" Preacher Green asked from behind Ty.

Jeff peeked through the part in the curtain. "Lexi's gettin' ready to try on the dress Freddie picked out." He clapped Ty on the back. "As soon as she gives the signal, we'll get this show on the road."

"Looks like everybody's here," Preacher Green announced when the back door opened and Martha hurried inside with the baby.

"I got here as soon as I could," Martha said, breathlessly. "Does Lexi suspect anything?"

Ty shook his head. "No. If she did, I'm sure she'd be out of here in a flash."

Martha placed a reassuring hand on Ty's arm. "Relax, Doc. If I wasn't sure this is the right thing to do, I wouldn't have any part in it."

"Martha's right," Jeff agreed. "Sometimes Lexi don't know beans from buckshot about what's good for her." His grin wide, he held up the shotgun. "That's why we've got ol' Betsy here. To convince her."

Ty looked from Jeff to Martha. He hoped like hell they were right.

"Freddie, I don't see any reason to try on these shoes," Lexi protested when her sister-in-law pushed a pair of ivory satin pumps into the tiny dressing cubicle.

"You have to," Freddie insisted.

"Why?"

Freddie blinked owlishly as if searching for an answer. "Because...because..." She looked at the elderly shop owner hovering beside her. "Feel free to jump in here anytime, Miss Eunice. Why does Lexi have to try on the shoes?"

The older woman stepped forward, her smile confident. "You have to put on the shoes so we can make sure the hem is just the right length, Lexi."

Lexi thought the reason sounded lame. But if it would hurry things along, she'd do whatever they asked. The sooner she finished trying on a dress she didn't want, need, or intend to buy, the sooner she could get back to the baby.

Slipping the pumps on, Lexi stepped out of the dressing room to stare at her image in the full-length mirror. She should have paid more attention to the dress Freddie had shoved into her hands and insisted she try on.

Made of soft ivory satin overlaid with delicate white lace, the garment had a sweetheart neckline, a dropped waist bodice adorned with seed pearls and a midcalf handkerchief hem. It was utterly stunning and looked just like a—

Lexi whirled around to face Freddie and Miss Eunice. "This is a wedding dress!"

"Oh, Lexi, it's perfect," Freddie exclaimed, tears filling her eyes. "You look beautiful."

"Let's see how these flowers look with the dress," Miss Eunice said.

Before Lexi could protest, the elderly woman shoved a bouquet of brightly colored wildflowers into her hands, plopped a matching garland on top of her head and fastened a string of pearls around her neck.

"What on earth—"

Lexi stopped short and blinked against the bright flashes of light as Freddie clicked off several pictures with the camera she'd pulled from her shoulder bag. Momentarily blinded and caught completely off guard, she teetered precariously when Freddie lifted her foot and slipped a blue garter up her leg to just above the knee.

Despite the fact that Lexi was off balance and seeing colorful spots dancing before her eyes, movement at the back of the shop caught her attention. She stared openmouthed at the sight of Ty, Jeff, Preacher Green and Martha, with the baby in tow, emerging single file from Miss Eunice's stockroom.

Lexi felt the blood drain from her face when she realized where they were headed.

Miss Eunice's wedding display, complete with fake marble columns, matching candelabras and brass arch, decorated with cheap plastic greenery, was ominously empty of its bride and groom mannequins.

Six

"**Y**ou're supposed to be a nervous bridegroom, Braden," Jeff said under his breath. "Act like one."

His hands raised in surrender, Ty felt a trickle of sweat make its way from his temple to the edge of his jaw as they marched toward the brass arch. "Believe me, that won't be much of a stretch."

"Lexi, get over here," Jeff bellowed. He poked Ty's back with the shotgun. "Braden and I had a long talk and he's finally come around to my way of thinkin'."

Ty glanced at Lexi and wished with all his heart he hadn't. He'd been right about her not liking the situation. In less than a split second, her expression had changed from shock to absolute fury.

Oh, he hadn't deluded himself into thinking she'd readily embrace the idea of a shotgun wedding. At first, he hadn't either. But when Martha took it upon herself to mention the scheme to Jeff and Freddie, the three had presented a very convincing argument. Once they were legally married, Ty would not only get to be a full-time father, he and Lexi might be more inclined to renew their acquaintance and explore what they might have had together if she'd remained in Chicago.

At the time it seemed the perfect solution. Now it sounded like the most ridiculous scheme he'd ever heard.

Marriage was a hard enough proposition when both parties were willing. But a forced marriage? And a groom with a past that the bride might never be able to understand or forgive?

"Jeff, have you lost your mind?" Lexi shrieked, drawing Ty back to the present. "Put that gun down."

"No way." Jeff motioned for Ty to take his place beneath the vine-covered arch. "Braden's gonna do what he should have in the first place. He's gonna do right by you and the baby."

Lexi turned her furious gaze on Freddie. "You obviously had a hand in all of this. I don't suppose I can count on you to talk some sense into that bone-headed brother of mine?"

Freddie looked anything but repentant. "Nope." She put her arm around Lexi's shoulders to urge her forward. "We've all talked it over and everybody agreed. The three of you need to be a family."

Lexi felt color flood her cheeks as she watched Martha, Preacher Green and Miss Eunice bob their heads in complete agreement. "They were in on this, too?"

"You bet." Martha looked proud as punch. "I'm the one who suggested it."

"Well, it's not going to work," Lexi retorted. She threw the bouquet at Freddie and moved to take the baby from Martha. "Matthew and I are going home. And if you're all lucky, I may forget all this in about fifty years."

"Don't even think about it, Sis," Jeff said, his expression grim. He drew back first one hammer on the gun, then the other. "At this range, I could hit Braden with both eyes closed."

The sound stopped Lexi in her tracks. "Jeff Hatfield, you wouldn't dare."

He gave her a one-shouldered shrug as he continued to aim the gun at Ty's back. "Try me."

"Under the circumstances, I'd rather you didn't test him, Lexi," Ty said through clenched teeth.

Lexi bit her lower lip to keep from uttering a most unladylike word in front of Preacher Green. She turned her attention back to the gun Jeff held. She didn't think he would carry through on his threat. But she wasn't sure. Jeff had an unshakable opinion of right and wrong when it came to marriage and babies. If he'd made up his mind that Ty should marry her, nothing would change it.

Her gaze narrowed on Ty. His voice sounded surprisingly calm, all things considered. As a doctor, surely he'd seen the damage a shotgun could do. If he had any sense he should be scared half out of his mind. But to her way of thinking, he looked a little too composed for a man with a double-barrel poking him in the back.

"You're willing to go through with this?" she asked him.

Ty glanced over his shoulder at the gun Jeff held,

then back at her. His smile tense, he nodded. "More than willing."

Freddie took advantage of Lexi's hesitation. "See, Lex. He wants to marry you." She shoved the wildflowers into Lexi's hands and pushed her forward. Whispering close to her ear, Freddie added, "Here's your chance for the happily-ever-after you always talked about when we were kids."

Lexi glared at her sister-in-law. "I'll never tell you another thing as long as I live. In fact, you'll be lucky if I ever speak to you again."

"Oh, you'll talk to me." Freddie laughed as she positioned Lexi next to Ty beneath the arch. "And I'm bettin' it won't be too long before you're fallin' all over yourself to say thanks, too."

"Don't hold your breath," Lexi muttered.

"This is truly a joyous day," Preacher Green pronounced, stepping in front of Lexi and Ty.

"I just love weddins," Miss Eunice blubbered into her lace-edged hanky.

"Aw, shut up, Eunice," Martha said, her own voice quavering. "Let Preacher Green get the deed done before one of these two bolts for the door."

"Dearly beloved…"

Ty's chest tightened when he looked at his beautiful bride. He'd have liked to start their union on better terms. But since that didn't seem possible, Ty would take what he could get and hope their differences could be worked out later.

"Join hands and face each other as you repeat after me," Preacher Green commanded.

Ty watched Lexi hand her bouquet to Freddie, then turn to face him. Her green eyes sparkled with anger and her slender fingers trembled, but she didn't hesitate. When she placed her hands in his, he felt like he'd been handed a rare and precious gift.

"I, Tyler Braden, take thee, Lexi Hatfield—"

Lexi listened to Ty's rich baritone as he repeated the sacred vows. His strong, sure hands wrapped protectively around hers, his warm smile as he gazed down at her, made her insides feel warm and quivery.

She mentally gave herself a good shaking. That didn't change one darned thing. As soon as they were finished, she fully intended to walk right out of Miss Eunice's Dress Shop and straight across the street to the office of Warren Jacobs, Attorney at Law.

"The ring, please?" Preacher Green requested.

Smiling in spite of her tears, Martha stepped forward with Matthew. "Not every little boy will be able to say he was the ring bearer at his mama and daddy's weddin'."

That was when Lexi noticed the matching gold wedding bands tied to the slender white ribbons of the baby's sacque. The sight caused her own tears to threaten as she watched Ty unfasten one of the rings and take her hand in his.

"With this ring…"

His gaze held her captive while he pledged his faithfulness and slipped the wide band over her finger. When he tenderly rubbed the pad of his thumb over the shiny gold, warming the ring—warming her—Lexi's toes curled inside the ivory pumps.

She jerked her hand from his. She'd better watch it. His touch could almost soften her resolve. And she fully intended to see the marriage annulled before the ink had a chance to dry on the certificate.

Preacher Green cleared his throat for the second time.

"Lexi?"

His smile warm, Ty extended his left hand. "Your turn."

Lexi blinked. She'd been so caught up in her own thoughts, she'd lost track of what would happen next.

Her hands trembled as she unfastened Ty's ring from the ribbon on Matthew's short jacket and tersely repeated the words everyone expected to hear. But the moment she slipped the ring on Ty's finger and he closed his hands over hers, her pulse took off at a gallop and her breath came in short little puffs.

"By the power vested in me by God and the State of Tennessee, I now pronounce you husband and wife," Preacher Green said, sounding very pleased. "You may kiss the bride."

When Ty continued to gaze at her, Preacher Green chuckled and tapped him on the shoulder. "Kiss your bride, son."

Ty grinned, then gently drew her forward to seal their union with the traditional kiss. She watched him slowly, deliberately, lower his head until their lips met, his mouth covering hers in tender exploration.

Her legs began to tremble.

His tongue stroked her lips apart, then thrust inside in a possessive claiming.

Her knees failed completely.

When she sagged against him, he tightened his arms and drew her even closer. The feel of his obvious desire pressed to her lower belly caused her heart to race and her head to spin. Heat shot through her as he gently stroked her tongue with his, imitating the movements of more intimate lovemaking.

In the confines of her borrowed satin shoes, her toes curled, straightened and curled again.

"Save it for the honeymoon, Braden," Jeff said, pulling Lexi from Ty's arms. He wrapped her in a brotherly bear hug. "Congratulations, Sis."

Dazed from Ty's kiss, Lexi could only nod.

"I'm glad you finally caved in and went along with this," Jeff said close to her ear.

Lexi blinked as reality slowly returned. "Why?"

"Well, first of all, it was the right thing to do," he stated emphatically. "And second, it could have proven mighty embarrassin'."

She pulled back to meet her brother's relieved gaze. "What on earth are you talking about, Jeff?"

"I don't know what I would have done if you'd recognized ol' Betsy," he admitted.

Lexi stared at the gun in Jeff's hands. "You mean you forced us to get married with a shotgun that won't even fire?"

Jeff nodded, his grin wide. "You didn't think I'd take the chance on turnin' you into a widow before you became a wife, did you?"

"I swear if it's the last thing I do, I'll get even with you for this, Jeff Hatfield," Lexi said. Fixing her gaze on the lawyer's office across the street, she marched toward the door.

Dixie Ridge seemed strangely vacant when Ty steered the SUV away from the curb in front of Miss Eunice's Dress Shop. The old shoes and tin cans tied to the back of the truck thumped and pinged the pavement, the sound amplified by the unnatural quiet.

Ty barely noticed.

His attention was focused on the silent woman beside him. Lexi's pensive mood bothered him. She hadn't said two words to him since Preacher Green pronounced them husband and wife. Was she already trying to think of a way to get out of their marriage?

Freddie had assured him Lexi would protest, but once she'd said her vows, she'd do her best to stick to them. Had Freddie been wrong?

Or did Lexi think he felt trapped? Should he admit that it had all been a setup? That he'd willingly gone along with the plan? That he'd even insisted the wedding date be set far enough past the baby's birth so they could have a real wedding night?

As he turned the truck onto the road leading up the side of the mountain, Ty weighed his options. Maybe he'd tell her on their fiftieth wedding anniversary, but he didn't think it would be wise to inform her of the ruse now.

He reached for her hand to reassure himself she really was seated beside him. He smiled when his thumb grazed the gold band he'd recently placed on his wife's finger.

His wife.

Ty liked the sound of those words. He'd long ago given up on ever having a wife and family, wouldn't allow himself to think about something he knew he could never have. Now it seemed a very real possibility, and what he wanted more than he could have ever imagined.

"I don't know much about being a husband and father," he admitted to the silent woman beside him. "But I promise, I'll do my best. We can make this work, Lexi."

Lexi tensed at the sincerity she detected in Ty's voice. He sounded as if he wanted them to stay together. Nothing would make her happier than to have a loving husband and a good father for Matthew.

Play **LUCKY HEARTS** for this...

exciting FREE gift!
This surprise mystery gift could be yours free

when you play **LUCKY HEARTS!**
...then continue your lucky streak with a sweetheart of a deal!

1. Play Lucky Hearts as instructed on the opposite page.

2. Send back this card and you'll receive 2 brand-new Silhouette Desire® novels. These books have a cover price of $3.99 each in the U.S. and $4.50 each in Canada, but they are yours to keep absolutely free.

3. There's no catch! You're under no obligation to buy anything. We charge nothing—ZERO—for your first shipment. And you don't have to make any minimum number of purchases—not even one!

4. The fact is thousands of readers enjoy receiving their books by mail from the Silhouette Reader Service™. They enjoy the convenience of home delivery...they like getting the best new novels at discount prices, BEFORE they're available in stores...and they love their *Heart to Heart* subscriber newsletter featuring author news, horoscopes, recipes, book reviews and much more!

5. We hope that after receiving your free books you'll want to remain a subscriber. But the choice is yours—to continue or cancel, any time at all! So why not take us up on our invitation, with no risk of any kind. You'll be glad you did!

Visit us online at
www.eHarlequin.com

The Silhouette Reader Service™—Here's how it works:

Accepting your 2 free books and gift places you under no obligation to buy anything. You may keep the books and gift and return the shipping statement marked "cancel." If you do not cancel, about a month later we'll send you 6 additional novels and bill you just $3.34 each in the U.S., or $3.74 each in Canada, plus 25¢ shipping & handling per book and applicable taxes if any.* That's the complete price and — compared to cover prices of $3.99 each in the U.S. and $4.50 each in Canada — it's quite a bargain! You may cancel at any time, but if you choose to continue, every month we'll send you 6 more books, which you may either purchase at the discount price or return to us and cancel your subscription.

*Terms and prices subject to change without notice. Sales tax applicable in N.Y. Canadian residents will be charged applicable provincial taxes and GST.

If offer card is missing write to: Silhouette Reader Service, 3010 Walden Ave., P.O. Box 1867, Buffalo, NY 14240-1867

SILHOUETTE READER SERVICE
3010 WALDEN AVE
PO BOX 1867
BUFFALO NY 14240-9952

BUSINESS REPLY MAIL
FIRST-CLASS MAIL   PERMIT NO. 717   BUFFALO, NY

POSTAGE WILL BE PAID BY ADDRESSEE

NO POSTAGE
NECESSARY
IF MAILED
IN THE
UNITED STATES

She glanced over at the profile of her handsome husband. In the weeks following their son's birth, she'd witnessed firsthand that Ty was a good, caring father. But a loving husband? Oh, she knew he was as attracted to her as she was to him. But that didn't mean they'd be able to build a lasting relationship. And a marriage at gunpoint wasn't the same as starting a life together based on love and mutual respect. Besides, he'd be going back to Chicago and she had no intention of returning to the city. She wanted to raise Matthew right here in the mountains of Tennessee. It would be best for all concerned to end the marriage with a quiet annulment before news of the wedding had a chance to get out. She'd already have things underway if Warren Jacobs's office hadn't been closed on Saturdays.

"What the hell is this all about?" Ty asked, drawing her out of her pensive mood.

He'd turned the truck into the drive leading up to her cabin, but the narrow lane was blocked by a horse-drawn carriage with a "Just Hitched" sign attached to the back.

When Ty stopped the SUV, Harv Jenkins jumped down from the front seat of the surrey and motioned for Ty to roll down the window. "Afternoon, Doc," he said, tipping his hat. "Just park over to the side of the driveway and I'll give you and the new Missus a ride up to the house." His toothless grin wide, he added, "You make a mighty pretty bride, Miss Lexi."

"What's going on?" Ty asked, parking the truck where Harv indicated.

"I'm not sure." Lexi got out of the truck and slammed the door as Jeff pulled his truck in behind the carriage. She pointed a finger at her brother and

Freddie, who got out to drive the SUV up to the cabin. "Those two are toast. When they insisted the baby had to ride with them, I should have known they had something else up their sleeves."

Ty helped her get seated in the carriage, then slid in beside her. "What do you think they're up to now?"

"No good, if I know that brother of mine," Lexi stated flatly.

Harv slapped the big, gray horse on the rump with the reins and the carriage lurched forward. The rollicking sounds of music and laughter reached them just before they rounded the curve in the lane and pulled to a stop at the edge of Lexi's yard.

"It looks like a carnival," Ty grumbled.

Struck speechless by the large crowd milling around her yard, Lexi could only nod. In little more than an hour, her tidy lawn had been turned into an elaborate outdoor wedding reception.

White crepe paper streamers and expandable tissue bells hung from every tree. Tables and chairs, borrowed from the Methodist church down in town, had been set up banquet fashion in front of a head table. They'd been decorated with wildflower centerpieces that matched the bouquet she still held.

More than a little dazed, Lexi watched the edge of a long, white tablecloth flutter in the breeze. The buffet table, piled high with assorted dishes and platters of delicious-smelling homemade food, had been constructed of sawhorses and a sheet of plywood. Similar tables had been set up to hold a huge punch bowl, wedding cake and gifts. Her neighbors had even taken down the wooden swing on her front porch in order to make room for a small band.

She might have found it all very touching had she not felt as if her life had gone into a flat spin with no hope of recovery. This morning she'd been a single mother with nothing more on her mind than trying to get out of a shopping trip with her persistent sister-in-law. Now she found herself married, facing a wedding reception that looked as if it could go on well into the night, and forced into altering her annulment plans.

Her idea of keeping things quiet had just been blown to smithereens. With the whole mountain celebrating her nuptials, there was no way she could end the charade of a marriage now. She'd already fed the local gossips enough ammunition when she came home pregnant from Chicago. They'd all called her "that poor little gal up on Piney Knob some city slicker led astray." She certainly didn't intend to give them reason to start up the rumor mill again.

"I don't remember this being part of the plan," Ty muttered.

"What was that?" Lexi asked, distracted. With all of her neighbors descending on the carriage, she wasn't sure she'd heard him correctly.

He cleared his throat. "I said, I don't remember seeing such a clan."

She gave him a suspicious look. Something told her he knew a whole lot more about the day's events than a groom at a shotgun wedding should. But she didn't have time to dwell on the fact. A stream of well-wishers surrounded the carriage and before she knew what was happening, Ty jumped to the ground and helped her down.

His hands still at her waist, Ty watched the crowd part to allow an old woman the honor of being the first to congratulate the bride and groom. "Lexi, you're just about the prettiest bride I ever did see," the old woman stated. She wrapped Lexi in a loving embrace, then stepped back, her gaze raking Ty from head to toe. "Boy, you don't hardly look old enough to spawn a baby, let alone help birth one."

Lexi laughed. "Ty, this is Granny Applegate."

He stared in disbelief at the tiny, old woman in front of him. When he'd first heard of Granny Applegate, he'd pictured an old crony in a flowing black cape, with stringy gray hair and a wart on the end of her nose. But in reality, the elderly lady wore a brightly colored housedress, had short, snow-white curls and one of the kindest faces he'd ever seen.

"Boy, if you don't shut your mouth right quick, you're gonna catch a bug," Granny cackled.

"It's nice to meet you," he said, finally getting his vocal cords to work.

She patted his arm with a bony hand, her smile warm. "Later on, me and you are gonna have a talk, son."

"We are?"

Granny nodded so vigorously, her white curls bobbed. "I'm gettin' on in years and I'm thinkin' you might be a good one to take over birthin' the babies here on Piney Knob. But we'll talk about that some other time." She patted his arm again. "Welcome to the mountain, son."

Ty didn't have time to tell the old woman he'd be leaving in a few short months. For the next twenty minutes, he and Lexi were deluged with neighbors and friends expressing their heartfelt congratulations.

"You've got to see the decorations," one of the women said, tugging Lexi from his side.

He regretfully watched a group of women lead his new wife across the yard to show her their handiwork. When Jeff and Freddie insisted they take the baby for the evening so he and Lexi could be alone, he had immediately started making plans for their wedding night. And they definitely hadn't included a large, boisterous crowd.

"I wish you'd told me when I was at the clinic last month that you were lookin' for a wife," a young woman said, sauntering up to him. She pursed her bright red lips in an obviously well-practiced pout, batted her false eyelashes and ran a perfectly manicured, fake red fingernail along the satin lapel of his tux. "I'd have been more than happy to apply for the job."

Ty was saved from having to comment when Jeff came to stand beside him. "Mary Ann, I saw Jake Sanders over by the punch bowl a few minutes ago. He was lookin' mighty lonely and I think I heard him ask where you were." Jeff winked as he place Matthew into Ty's arms.

The dark-haired young woman brightened instantly. "See you later, boys," she called, hurrying across the yard.

"Thanks," Ty said, grateful for Jeff's intervention. He cradled his son to his chest as he watched Mary Ann zero in on her next unsuspecting victim. "Don't you think one of us should warn Jake?"

"Naw. Those two have been carryin' on for years." Jeff chuckled as they watched the voluptuous woman separate Jake from the group of men standing around the punch bowl, take him by the hand and hurry him into the woods. "One of these days he'll get up the nerve to ask her to marry him. Then all the men on the mountain can breathe easy again.''

''I know of at least one wife who'll be glad to see that happen,'' Freddie added from her husband's side.

''Now, darlin', you know you don't have a thing to worry about,'' Jeff said, draping his arm around Freddie's shoulders. ''I'm a one-woman man.'' He kissed the top of her head. ''And you're the only woman for me.''

Ty felt a stab of envy at their affectionate banter. Would Lexi feel the same when the flirtatious woman was no longer single? Did she even care that Mary Ann had openly flirted with him?

Mary Ann Simmons leaned her full bosom against Ty and Lexi saw red. Mary Ann could flirt with every other man on the mountain in her attempt to get Jake Sanders to propose, but she'd better leave Ty alone. Lexi wasn't sure why she felt that way, since she had no intention of staying married to the man. But that didn't matter. Right now Ty *was* her husband.

Her husband.

She still couldn't believe she and Ty were married. But thanks to her brother's highhandedness, she now found herself legally wed to the father of her child. And by forcing the marriage, Jeff had unwittingly added one more obstacle for them to overcome before they could reach an amicable agreement on joint custody of Matthew.

Lexi watched Ty hold their son as he talked with Jeff and Freddie. He looked completely at ease and not at all like a man who had just been forced into doing something he didn't want to do.

The baby wrapped his fingers around one of Ty's and she watched him smile down at their son. They were forming a strong bond, and one that she hoped would remain strong after Ty went back to Chicago.

Lost in thought, it took her a moment to realize someone was ringing a bell. The majority of the crowd soon produced bells of their own and joined in. Lexi suddenly found herself being ushered to the middle of the yard.

"They won't stop until you two kiss," Helen McKinney told Ty. She gave Lexi a conspiratorial wink. "And it better be a good one."

Lexi watched her brother nudge Ty. Nodding, he shrugged out of the tux jacket, handed it to Jeff, then rolled up the sleeves on his white shirt. He started toward her, and as he drew closer, her heart skipped a beat. His eyes had darkened to navy, and the promising smile curving his firm lips took her breath away.

The crowd closed in for a better look when Ty stepped close and folded her into his arms. His strength held her captive, his warmth surrounded her, making her legs tremble.

Lexi placed her hands on Ty's broad chest to steady herself. If her knees didn't stop wobbling, she'd have to have the problem checked out by a doctor.

Her stomach fluttered wildly as an image of Ty's strong, talented hands gliding along her legs flashed through her mind.

"Are you two gonna moon-eye each other all day?" someone shouted.

"Plant one on her, Doc," Harv urged. "We ain't gonna stop ringin' these bells till you do."

Ty gazed down at Lexi a moment before dipping

his head to do as the crowd requested. Slowly, thoroughly, he tasted her peach-flavored lip gloss, savored her tenderness as she returned his caress. His tongue coaxed, teased, then parted her lips to enter the sweet, warm recesses of her mouth.

He tried to remind himself they were standing in front of at least a hundred people. His body could have cared less. Her soft sigh as he deepened the kiss, her tongue stroking his, caused heat to gather in his loins and his body to strain against the fabric of his trousers.

"Way to go, Doc!" a teenage boy yelled.

Lexi started to pull away, but Ty held her close. "Give me a minute," he said, his voice husky.

"What's wrong?" she asked, her breasts brushing his chest as they rose and fell with her labored breathing.

"Just stay close," he whispered against her hair. The smell of her honeysuckle shampoo teased his nostrils and Ty pulled back to keep from making matters worse. "Something came up," he growled.

Lexi's eyes twinkled. "Oh, really? And what would that be, Dr. Braden?"

Feeling his body begin to relax, Ty gave her a quick, hard kiss, then set her away from him. His grin wicked, he promised, "I'll show you later, *Mrs. Braden.*"

Seven

Ty stood on the porch beside Lexi as they waved goodbye to the last of their guests. He'd really enjoyed getting better acquainted with the people of Piney Knob. He liked watching them leave even more.

He'd wanted to be alone with Lexi all day. But once started, the wedding reception seemed to go on forever. And it might have, if not for Carl Morgan's very pregnant wife, Lydia, going into labor.

For the first time since arriving in the mountains, Ty was glad to hear the woman preferred Granny Applegate attending to the delivery and not him. He had plans for the rest of the evening, and they certainly didn't include using his medical degree.

"Do you think Matthew will be all right?" Lexi asked, giggling.

He watched the taillights of Jeff and Freddie's car

disappear around the bend in the drive. "Matthew will be just fine with your brother and Freddie. If they need us, they'll call."

Lexi hiccuped, then in a stage whisper added, "I'm a little tipsy. I think someone might have spiked the punch."

"I don't think they did, honey, I *know* they did." He placed his arm around her shoulders and steered her into the house.

Throughout the day, Carl Morgan and Harv Jenkins dug into their coat pockets for fruit jars filled with moonshine, which they poured into the frothy orange punch. Fortunately, when Mary Ann Simmons separated Jake Sanders from the pack of men guarding the large bowl, Ty noticed what was taking place. From that point on, he'd opted to drink iced tea instead.

He closed the door and secured the lock before turning to face Lexi. He didn't want her to get the idea he was rushing her, but the day had taken its toll. Throughout the afternoon and well into the evening, he'd held Lexi close, kissed her when the crowd rang the bells, and ached a little more each time he had to let her go.

"Come here, Mrs. Braden," he said, reaching for her.

"Ty, we need to talk—"

"Not tonight, honey." Pulling her close, he buried his face in her honeysuckle-scented hair. "I've had a hell of a day and talking isn't what's going to make it better."

Ty's lips caressed her temple, her ear, then trailed tiny kisses to the wildly fluttering pulse at the base of her throat. She'd had just enough punch to make her brain foggy and her will to resist him almost powerless.

He tightened his embrace and the evidence of his hunger pressing against her lower belly made her tingle all over. His spicy aftershave intoxicated her with its musky scent. The knot of desire, building inside her from the moment he sealed their union with a kiss at the end of their marriage ceremony, tightened into an almost painful ache. He lowered his lips to hers in a kiss so tender, it brought tears to her eyes. The feel of his tongue claiming hers sent heat coursing through her veins.

Just when she thought she would surely go into total meltdown, Ty ended the kiss. Taking her hand in his, he started toward the hall.

"Let's go to bed, Mrs. Braden."

Lexi allowed Ty to lead her down the hall and into her bedroom. Her heart and traitorous body told her to throw caution to the wind and make love with her husband. Her fuzzy mind tried to remind her they wouldn't be married long, but for the life of her, she couldn't remember why.

He stopped to turn on the lamp beside the bed. His smile promising, he reached out to trace his finger along the lace edge of her neckline. "This dress is beautiful, but I'm sure it will look much nicer hanging in the closet."

His low, soft-spoken comment made her heart skip a beat. Consummating their marriage would only add more complications, but the combination of Ty's lovemaking and the spiked punch put reason and logic beyond her capabilities.

He turned her away from him, arranged her hair over her shoulder and pulled down the zipper. The raspy sound caused tingles of anticipation to skip along every nerve ending in her body and she felt her knees begin to tremble.

Ty pressed his lips to her nape as he slid his hands inside the dress to caress her shoulders, then slowly eased the garment down her arms. Tremors of excitement coursed through her and her breathing became shallow at his featherlight touch.

When the dress lay around her feet in a pool of shiny satin and frothy lace, Ty wrapped his arms around her to pull her back against him. The feel of his solid frame, the scent of his musky cologne, caused heat to pool deep in her belly. When her head fell back against his shoulder, he pressed tiny kisses to the exposed column of her neck.

"Ty..."

"Yes."

"The light..."

"What about it?" he asked, his arms wrapping around her as he continued to nibble his way across her shoulder.

"Please, turn it off."

His cheek pressed close to her ear, he whispered, "You weren't shy with me before, honey. What's wrong?"

Her breath caught as his hands slid down the length of her sides, then back up to the swell of her breasts. "I...was in shape then."

"Honey, you're more beautiful today than the day we met," he said, his voice husky. Reaching out, he switched off the lamp. "But I want you to feel comfortable with me."

Lost in the sound of his deep voice and the feel of his firm lips on her sensitive skin, Lexi couldn't have responded if her life depended on it. Muted light from the sliver of moon outside intimately surrounded them, and the warmth of Ty's hands closing over her breasts caused waves of longing to course through her. She briefly wondered when he'd removed the rest of her clothing, but when he turned her to face him, the sight of hungry desire in his navy eyes and the sound of his ragged breathing stole her breath.

She ran her fingernail over one of the shiny black studs holding his shirt closed. "You looked very handsome in this tux today, Dr. Braden."

Ty's body tightened further with each one of Lexi's throaty words. He'd wanted to take things slow, to make their first time together as man and wife very special. But the velvet rasp of desire in her voice very nearly sent him over the edge.

Impatient to feel her silky skin against his own, he brushed her fingers aside, grasped the edges of the shirt and tugged. Polished black studs flew in all directions. He couldn't have cared less. He pulled her to him and the feel of her firm breasts heating his chest, her hardened nipples pressing into his skin, had him thinking he just might have a coronary right then and there.

"Honey, this feels almost too good." He shuddered as he tried to catch hold of his rapidly deteriorating control. "It's been a long time. I'm not sure I'll be able to take things as slow as I had intended."

"Ty—"

Although she hadn't moved, he felt her withdrawal as surely as if she'd pulled from his arms. He knew what ran through her mind, the question she couldn't bring herself to ask.

He placed his finger beneath her chin and tilted her

head until their gazes locked. "There hasn't been anyone since you left Chicago, Lexi. You're the only woman I've made love to in the last year."

"Since that night," she whispered.

Nodding, he smiled. "That's right, honey. And I vowed today that you'll be the only woman for the rest of my life."

He lowered his head to seal the promise with a kiss and felt her apprehension drain away on a soft sigh.

"Ty."

His name on her lips, her warm breath feathering his skin as she spoke, had his body pulsing with urgent need. He moved them closer to the bed, but the tuxedo trousers slid down around his ankles, causing him to stumble. His arms still holding Lexi against him, they fell across the four-poster bed in an undignified heap.

No sooner had they landed on the mattress than a horrible clanging split the air.

"What the hell is that?" he asked, trying to kick free of the slacks. The more he struggled, the louder the noise became.

Lexi suddenly burst out laughing. "I'd wondered where Jeff and Freddie disappeared to right after the band started playing. Now I know."

With every clang, Lexi's laughter increased.

He stopped trying to free himself and gave her a suspicious look. The deafening sound quieted, but Lexi continued to laugh.

"Jeff…Freddie…cowbells," she gasped.

Ty frowned. She must have had more punch than he'd thought. "Lexi, honey, you're not making sense," he said patiently. "What do Jeff and Freddie have to do with cowbells?"

When she continued to laugh, he shifted to gaze down at her. His movement only caused the noise to begin again and her laughter to increase.

Tears rolled down Lexi's cheeks as she shook her head. "They tied cowbells…to the bottom of the bed."

"That's what the clanging is?"

She nodded and the noise commenced again. So did her laughter.

Ty cursed as he sat up and switched on the lamp. Wrestling his legs free of the slacks, he knelt down to peer under the bed. Over a dozen bells in assorted sizes dangled from the springs.

Stretching out on his back, he inched his way beneath the bed. "Why the hell would they tie cowbells to the bottom of the bed?"

Giggling, Lexi wrapped herself in the quilt and peered over the side of the mattress at him. "So we'd have to stop what we were doing and untie them. Harassing newlyweds on their wedding night is a mountain tradition."

He yanked the string free on the last bell and hauled himself from under the bed. "Why?"

"It has something to do with—"

"Causing a hell of a lot of frustration for the couple?"

She nodded, her grin wide. "It certainly seems to have worked in your case."

Ty rose to his feet, switched off the light, then hooked his thumbs in the waistband of his white cotton briefs. "Fortunately, I'm very resil—"

His words stopped abruptly at a horrendous sound from outside. "What now?" he bellowed, switching on the light again.

Lexi scrambled from the bed. "It's a shivaree."

"What the hell is a shivaree?" he shouted above the whoops, catcalls and banging of pots and pans coming from the yard.

"Another one of those mountain customs," she answered, rushing to collect her clothes. "Now quick, get dressed."

"What will it take to make them stop?"

"We'll have to go out onto the front porch to greet the crowd," she said, sounding breathless from her haste to get dressed.

Pulling on the tuxedo slacks, Ty muttered a phrase that would have blistered the ears of a seasoned sailor. "We've been with these people all day. Wasn't that enough? Surely they have love lives of their own. Why do they feel the need to ruin ours?"

"It's hard to explain," Lexi said, struggling to zip the dress Ty had removed earlier. "But I promise, this is the last of the harassment. A shivaree is the grand finale."

"Good. The sooner it's over, the sooner they leave." He fastened the waistband of his trousers, then grabbed her hand. "Come on. Let's get this over with."

Lexi trotted along behind him. Poor guy had no idea how the shivaree would end, or the lasting effects it would have. "Ty, you don't understand—"

"Hey, Doc, you're lookin' a mite flustered," Harv Jenkins shouted when Ty flung open the door.

"Where'd you leave your shirt, Doc?" someone else called.

"Why did the light keep goin' on and off?" Jeff asked, his grin knowing.

"Lexi, how did you manage to turn your dress inside out?'' Freddie asked. Her hazel eyes sparkling with mischief, she pointed to Lexi's right arm. ''And why is your bra hangin' from the sleeve?''

As the group howled with laughter, Lexi looked at Ty. He wore nothing more than the tuxedo trousers and a frown. Glancing down at her dress, she groaned. In her haste she'd not only put the garment on inside out, the hook of her bra had caught on a thread and hung from her shoulder like a droopy flag.

''What happens now?'' Ty asked.

She felt a stab of guilt at what was about to happen, but there wasn't a thing she could do to stop it. ''We either serve them all a drink or they'll ride you around the yard in a wheelbarrow—''

''If that's all it takes to get them to leave, I'll be more than happy to play this silly game,'' Ty said, releasing her hand and vaulting off the porch.

Lexi started to tell him how the ride would end, but he was immediately cut off from her, surrounded by the laughing crowd. She watched helplessly as they led him over to where Jeff stood holding the handles of a one-wheeled cart.

''He doesn't know what's going to happen, does he?'' Freddie asked, climbing the steps of the porch to stand next to Lexi.

Lexi shook her head and watched Ty allow the men to seat him in the wheelbarrow. ''He doesn't have a clue.''

Obviously shocked, Freddie asked, ''Why didn't you tell him?''

''I tried, but he was so intent on getting it over with, he wouldn't listen.''

''I figured he was in the dark about it when he

willingly jumped off the porch,'' Freddie said, laughing.

"Is Martha watching the baby?'' Lexi asked as the procession began.

Freddie nodded. "We dropped them off at our house. Jeff will take her home when we get back.''

Lexi watched Ty being wheeled around the yard in a random pattern. "He thinks they'll ride him around for a few minutes and that'll be it.''

Jeff pushed Ty in a wide sweep around the front yard, the crowd running along behind, laughing and banging their pots and pans. When the parade started around the side of the house toward the small creek at the back of her property, Lexi glanced at her sister-in-law. "Time for the main event.''

Freddie turned to enter the house. "I'll go get some towels.''

Lexi ran down the steps and headed in the direction the crowd had taken Ty. "And start the hot water running in the shower.''

Ty gripped the sides of the wheelbarrow and wondered if he had somehow been transported to the Twilight Zone. Since his arrival in Dixie Ridge, he'd encountered some rather strange differences in culture and traditions. But this was without a doubt the most bizarre.

His rear end bounced up, then landed hard on the metal bottom of the cart as the wild ride continued around the side of the house, toward the back of Lexi's property. The crowd's laughter seemed almost maniacal and they beat their pots and pans harder the closer they got to the creek. He felt a tingle of apprehension run the length of his spine.

Turning to look over his shoulder, he tried to shout above the noise. "Jeff, you want to turn this thing around?"

"Hang on, Braden," Jeff said, grinning. "It's just about over."

"That's what I'm afraid of," Ty ground out between bone-jarring bumps. They were getting closer to the ice-cold stream than he felt comfortable with, and he had a sinking feeling he knew exactly how this strange ritual would end.

Closing his eyes, he held his breath and braced himself for the inevitable.

Ty's teeth chattered and he shivered uncontrollably as he stood beneath the spray of hot water. Steam filled the shower stall and rolled out to fog every corner of the small bathroom. He didn't care. He was colder than he'd ever been in his life. And try as he might, he couldn't erase the feel of icy water closing around him.

He closed his eyes and tried to stop shivering as he mentally ran through every curse word he'd ever heard. That done, he made up a few new ones.

He'd had big plans for the evening. He'd wanted to make love to Lexi all through the night, to show her how good they could be together. But when the crowd dumped him into the cold mountain stream, that idea had come to a swift and frigid end.

His teeth clicked together as another wave of goose bumps rose to the surface of his chilled skin. He'd never been one to feel sorry for himself, but he couldn't seem to keep the gloomy thoughts at bay.

He opened his eyes and glanced back down at his lower body. He wondered if certain parts of his anatomy would ever function normally again. As a doctor, he knew they would. But as a man facing his wedding night with no hope of loving his wife properly, Ty couldn't keep from feeling morose.

Just as the water began to turn tepid, Lexi's shadow appeared on the other side of the frosted glass door. "Ty, are you ready to get out? I've put the electric blanket on the bed and turned it up to high. It should be warm now."

He hurriedly shut off the tap, stepped out of the shower and grabbed the towel she'd warmed in the clothes dryer. He vigorously rubbed his chilled skin with the heated terrycloth.

"Put this on," she commanded, handing him a bathrobe.

"N-no…w-way." He tried to sound firm, but his teeth clicked together like a set of the chattering choppers sold in novelty stores and his staunch refusal lost all effect.

"It's just from the bathroom to the bedroom," Lexi said patiently. She draped the robe around his shoulders, then winked. "Besides, I promise not to tell your patients how good you look in pink chenille."

Ty might have protested further, but she'd heated the robe with the towel and he couldn't bear to give up the warmth it provided. "Th-thank y-you."

Once he was settled beneath the layers of several quilts and the electric blanket, his teeth still chattered, but his body was racked with only an occasional chill.

Lexi lay down beside him and snuggled close to share her body heat.

Nothing.

He pulled her closer.

His mind responded. His body remained dormant.

When she moved against him, Ty ground his teeth. He hated to admit it. It just wasn't something a man wanted to think about. Ever. And especially on his wedding night. But he might as well face facts. There was no way in hell his traumatized body was going to perform.

"Lexi, honey, I..." He paused as he searched for a less humiliating reason than admitting his predicament. Closing his eyes, he groaned. "I have a headache."

Eight

At the first ring of the phone, Ty reached across Lexi to the bedside table. He'd learned during the early days of his internship to awaken clearheaded and completely alert. His profession demanded it. All too often the snap decisions he had to make meant the difference between life and death.

"Dr. Braden speaking," he said, keeping his voice low. He didn't want to disturb Lexi.

"Doc, I know this is your weddin' night, and I hate to do this to you, but you're needed up here at the Morgan place," Martha said. "Granny ran into some problems. She called me to come help, but there's nothin' I can do. The baby's breech."

Ty looked at the clock and groaned. Why did so many infants decide to make their grand entrance at two or three in the morning?

After questioning Martha about the woman's condition, he determined it would be safe to move her. "Have Carl take her to the clinic," he said, throwing the covers back and sitting up on the side of the bed. "If the baby doesn't turn and Lydia can't deliver naturally, I may have to perform a C-section. If that happens, I want a sterile environment."

Martha's voice was all business. "We'll meet you at the clinic and I'll get things set up."

He once again glanced at the clock and did a quick mental calculation. "I should be there in fifteen minutes."

Hanging up the cordless phone, Ty glanced down at Lexi. She looked beautiful in sleep. Her long, dark lashes rested on her porcelain cheeks like tiny, wispy feathers. He wanted to kiss them. Her golden brown hair spread out across the pillow made him want to run his fingers through the silky strands as he made slow, passionate love to her. He felt his body react.

Great. Now that his body had finally thawed out and he experienced the first stirrings of desire, he had to go deliver a baby. Shaking his head, he slowly rose to his feet. "Some wedding night."

"Ty?" Lexi murmured sleepily. "Is it Freddie calling about Matthew?"

"The baby's fine," he said, pulling on the tuxedo trousers. He had no choice but to wear the ill-fitting suit. It was all he had to put on. He'd planned to move his things from the small apartment he'd rented above the Blue Bird Cafe sometime later today. Now he wished he'd thought to throw a pair of jeans and a T-shirt in the truck before the wedding yesterday.

"What's wrong?" she asked, sitting up.

"Granny can't deliver Lydia Morgan's baby," Ty said, stuffing the shirttail into his pants. "It's a breech presentation and I may have to perform an emergency Cesarean.''

Lexi pushed the hair from her eyes and got out of bed. "I'm going with you."

"There's no sense in you missing sleep," he argued. "If everything goes well, I should be back in a few hours."

"I want to go," she said. Rummaging around in the closet, she selected a pair of jeans and a light-weight sweater. "I might be able to help."

Ty caught her around the waist and pulled her to him. "Honey, Martha and I will take care of Lydia." He gave her a quick kiss. "There's nothing you can do."

"You don't know Carl," she argued, stepping back and heading for the bathroom. "He acts first and thinks about it later. I'll try to keep him in the waiting room, and have fresh coffee ready for anyone who wants it."

When she returned, Ty watched her tie her sneakers, then put her hair up in a ponytail. "Are you sure?" he asked, stepping into his own shoes.

"Yes."

Maybe if he allowed her to see what his job entailed, she'd better understand the times when he'd be called away or have to work terribly long hours. Smiling, he planted a quick kiss on her lips and threaded his arm through hers. "Come on. Let's go deliver a baby."

"Carl, I'm sure everything is going well," Lexi said, watching the big man pace the length of the waiting area.

She'd already had to talk him out of barging into

the tiny operating room once. She seriously doubted she could prevent him from entering the room if he really set his mind to it.

"Ty will do everything he can for Lydia and the baby," she said, hoping Carl listened.

When he turned to face her, his shoulders slumped and his brown eyes reflected the depth of his anguish. "I love Liddy more than life itself. If somethin' happens to her, I'll never forgive myself."

Envy pierced Lexi's heart. Why couldn't she have a relationship like that?

Restless, she left her chair. "Let's step outside and get a breath of fresh air, Carl. Maybe you'll feel a little better."

"But what if they need me?"

"Ty will send Martha to find you if something happens," Lexi said, pushing open the glass door that led to the parking lot.

As they stood watching signs of the approaching dawn, the inky darkness of the night sky dulled to the pale gray of early morning and the stars above seemed to blink out one by one. The lights over in the Blue Bird Cafe came on. Helen McKinney had arrived to start baking biscuits and making gravy for the breakfast crowd.

"Miss Lexi?"

She turned her attention back to the man beside her. "Feeling better, Carl?"

He took a deep shuddering breath. "If y'all don't mind, could I be by myself for a few minutes?" he asked, his voice rough with emotion.

"Of course, Carl." She reached out to touch his arm. "I'll be in the waiting room."

Tears blurring her vision, Lexi pushed through the

clinic door. She didn't have to look back to know that Carl had already knelt down, clasped his hands in front of him and thrown back his head to face the heavens as he prayed for his wife and unborn child.

It was clear Carl Morgan loved Lydia with all his heart and the possibility of something happening to his wife had literally brought the big man to his knees.

Lexi had always wanted a relationship like that, wanted her husband to love her with all his heart and soul. But thanks to her brother and his meddling ways, she found herself married to a man she hardly knew.

Oh, she'd always been attracted to Ty and he'd made no secret of the fact that the attraction was mutual. But that wasn't the same as love.

She pulled a tissue from the box on the reception counter and wiped the tears from her cheeks. Ty had made it clear that he intended to be a good husband and father and that he wanted them to stay married.

Lexi had no doubt that she could grow to love Ty. Just watching the way he cared for their son, she wasn't far from the emotion now. But would Ty ever be able to love her in return? He wanted to be a part of Matthew's life, but that didn't mean he wanted to be a part of hers as well. They'd married because he'd had a shotgun to his back, not because he'd fallen in love with her. Should she try, for their son's sake, to make their marriage work? Would that be enough for her?

"Martha, mark the time of birth," Ty said, placing the newborn across Lydia's stomach.

"Is my baby all right?" Lydia asked, her voice weak.

"Everything is fine," Ty assured her. "You have a beautiful daughter."

"Oh my!" Tears coursed down the woman's cheeks. "I've waited so long for a girl."

Ty smiled against the paper mask as he finished the postpartum procedures. Fortunately, the baby had turned herself in the womb and Lydia had delivered naturally.

"How many brothers does she have?" he asked.

"Five," Lydia said proudly.

Ty chuckled. "A basketball team."

Martha wrapped the baby in a pink receiving blanket, then placed her in her mother's arms. She took hold of the gurney to wheel it into one of the patient rooms at the back of the clinic. "Looks like you're startin' on the cheerleadin' squad now, Liddy."

"Oh, no I'm not," Lydia said, shaking her head. "After what I went through this time, there won't be a next time. Carl's gonna get fixed."

While Martha settled their patient in her room, Ty removed the mask and headed for the waiting area. Smiling, he shook his head. He didn't blame the woman after the difficult time she'd had giving birth, but he wondered if Carl would be all that eager to go along with his wife's solution to family planning.

"Where's Carl?" he asked, entering the small waiting area. Lexi sat by herself, her arms wrapped protectively around her middle.

"He stepped outside for some air." She rose to stand in front of him. "He's been half out of his mind with worry. It was all I could do to keep him out of there."

Ty nodded. He wanted to take her in his arms and ask what was wrong, why she looked at him with such sadness. But he needed to find Carl and alleviate the man's fears about Lydia. "I'll go talk to him."

"How did things go?"

"Everything went just fine." His gaze zeroed in on the plain gold band circling her left finger. For some reason, he'd needed the assurance that she still wore his ring. "I'll tell you all about it after I've talked to Carl."

Ty stepped out into the pale light of dawn and, glancing around, found Carl on his knees a few feet from the door, his wide shoulders shaking with silent sobs. Ty hesitated as he thought of Lexi and their own son's recent birth. Until a month and a half ago, he hadn't given any thought to how he'd feel if a woman had a difficult time delivering his child. It simply hadn't been an issue. But now, for the first time in his life, Ty fully understood the agony the man must have gone through while awaiting word about his wife and baby.

"Carl?"

The man was on his feet immediately. Unashamed of the tears still coursing down his cheeks, he demanded, "How's Liddy? Is she—"

Smiling, Ty placed his hand on Carl's shoulder. It felt wonderful to be delivering good news for a change, instead of offering hollow condolences. "We didn't have to perform a C-section, Carl. Lydia delivered naturally. She and your daughter are waiting for you to come in and see them."

"Daughter?" Clearly shocked, Carl's eyes widened. "Well, I'll be damned. Liddy's been wantin' a little girl for years." He quickly wiped the moisture from his cheeks with his shirt sleeve, then stuck out his hand to clasp Ty's. "I sure do appreciate everything you did for them, Doc."

Ty shook his head when Carl vigorously pumped his arm. "No need to thank me. I'm glad I was here to help."

Carl's mouth split into a wide grin as he released Ty's hand and headed for the door. "I'll make sure you don't regret comin' to Dixie Ridge, Doc. I surely will."

Ty followed the man inside the clinic. Every time one of his patients said something similar, he ended up with jars of home-canned pickles and jellies, or cakes or pies. He had no idea what Carl would show up with in the next few days. But Ty had no doubt the man would find some way to convey his appreciation.

He shook his head and started for the waiting room where he'd left Lexi. If the good people of Dixie Ridge gave him a choice, he'd be happy to have some uninterrupted time alone with his wife.

"You can hang your clothes on this side," Lexi said, pointing to the space she'd created in the closet. She watched Ty hang several pairs of jeans where she'd indicated, before she turned to the dresser. "I'll clear a drawer for your other things, then go down to Jeff's and Freddie's to pick up the baby."

Her mind straying back to what she'd witnessed at the clinic, Lexi absently removed the contents of the drawer, while he finished hanging his shirts.

"Tired?" Ty asked, his arms coming from behind to pull her back against him.

Lexi's pulse quickened and her breath caught at the

feel of his solid chest against her back, the strength of his arms wrapped around her. "Ty, we need to talk," she said, her voice not nearly as convincing as she would have liked. She cleared her throat and tried again. "We both—"

"Not now, honey." Ty's lips caressed her ear. "We've been married almost twenty-four hours and it's past time we became man and wife."

Drawing from an inner strength she hadn't known she possessed, Lexi stepped away from him. "No, Ty."

"Why?"

She took a deep breath before she turned to face him. "We may be married, but we aren't going to become man and wife. After a reasonable amount of time, we'll quietly get the marriage annulled, then go on with our separate lives."

She watched a shadow of emotion cross his face a moment before he folded his arms over his wide chest. "That's not acceptable."

"Why?" she asked, incredulous. "You couldn't possibly be any happier than I am about being forced into this charade."

He shrugged. "I'm willing to give it a try."

Tears threatened, but she blinked them back. "I want more in my marriage than for my husband to just 'give it a try.' I want him to be committed to the relationship. To give all of himself, and to settle for no less from me." Lexi shook her head. "Ty, do you realize how little I even know about you?"

"That works both ways, Lexi," Ty said evasively.

She'd be darned if she let him dodge the issue this time. She waved her hand, encompassing the room. "Look around, Ty. My life is an open book. What you see in this room, and throughout this cabin, is who I am. Where I come from.'' She pointed to the bed. ''The antique quilt my great-grandmother made over fifty years ago says I'm sentimental. The cradle Matthew sleeps in has been in my family for five generations. That says I value tradition. The picture of my parents hanging in the living room says I'm proud to have been their daughter.'' She propped her fists on her hips. ''You're the one who never talks about your family or your background. I don't even know your parents' names. Have you even bothered to tell them about Matthew?''

He tilted his head to stare at the ceiling a moment, took a deep breath, then meeting her gaze, answered. ''My mother's name was Mary. She died while I was in med school.''

Lexi could tell by the pain she heard in his voice that they'd been close. ''I'm sorry. What happened?'' she asked quietly.

''She suffered a fatal head injury during a mugging.''

''Is that why you became a trauma specialist?''

He nodded. ''I'd been leaning toward specializing in emergency medicine, but that more or less finalized my decision.''

''What about your father? Is he still alive?''

''I don't know.'' Ty's expression changed from sadness, to self-protection, then to deep regret. ''I have no idea who the man was.''

Lexi felt his pain as deeply as if it were her own. ''You were—''

''A bastard.'' The edge in his voice made her wince.

''I was going to say illegitimate,'' she said gently.

Ty's hollow laughter echoed through the room. "That's the nicest way anyone's ever put it."

"You're ashamed of it?" she asked, unable to understand why he thought it mattered.

"I've learned to live with it," he answered, his tone guarded. "But when I was growing up, I also learned very quickly not to let the fact be known."

"You were taunted because of it?" she guessed, feeling as if her heart would break. The loneliness and hurt he must have suffered as a child had to have been devastating. "Children can be very cruel."

Ty shrugged. "They only repeated what they'd heard their parents call me."

"Things are different now, Ty. It's more acceptable for a woman to choose single motherhood."

"Yes. But thirty-five years ago it wasn't widely accepted," he reminded her. "Sure, times were changing, but not in the neighborhood where I grew up. I was the only kid on the block without a father."

"Did your mother—"

Ty nodded. "She knew who he was, but she never would tell me. Apparently, their relationship ended on bad terms. Whenever I asked about him, all she'd ever say was that he wasn't worth knowing." He gave her a meaningful look. "And she didn't bother telling him about me either."

Realization slammed into Lexi, taking her breath. "If you hadn't taken over the clinic—"

"History would have repeated itself," he finished for her. "I might never have known I had a son."

Lexi didn't hesitate. She stepped forward and wrapped her arms around his stiff shoulders. "I always intended for our son to know who you are and for the two of you to meet. But I wanted to wait until he was old enough to understand.''

''Does my less than complete pedigree bother you?'' he asked.

Lexi's gaze locked with his. She could tell by the intensity in his deep blue eyes that her answer mattered a great deal to him.

''No. Why should it?''

''I have no heritage to pass along to Matthew,'' he said cautiously. ''I didn't even know my maternal grandparents. They refused to have anything to do with me, or my mother. They said I was a constant reminder of the shame she'd brought to their family.''

Understanding suddenly dawned as she stared at him. ''That's the reason you never wanted to have children, isn't it? You didn't feel you had anything to offer them?''

He nodded. ''I have no idea what kind of genes I'll be passing on.''

''Ty, none of that will matter to Matthew,'' she said firmly. ''He'll love you for the man you are. All that will matter to him is that you return his love.''

Ty reached out to pull her to him. ''What about you, Lexi? How does it make you feel to know your husband is a—''

She placed her fingers to his lips to keep him from saying the ugly word. ''Don't ever call yourself that again.'' She searched his face. ''Why would I care?''

''I've only shared this with one other woman and her reaction was anything but understanding.''

Lexi couldn't believe that such a trivial thing as illegitimacy would matter to anyone. ''She was a complete fool.''

He let out a deep, shuddering breath. "It's a relief to have that out in the open."

Loosening her ponytail, he arranged her hair around her shoulders, then placed his forefinger beneath her chin. He tilted her head so their gazes met. "Please, Lexi, give our marriage a chance. Let me be part of a whole family for the first time in my life."

Lexi closed her eyes to his beseeching look. She felt like she was teetering on the edge of a cliff. The next step she took, whether forward or back, could very well be the biggest mistake of her life.

"I have another confession to make, honey." His lips tenderly skimmed her cheek. "At the wedding yesterday, I was a willing participant. You were the only one present who didn't have prior knowledge of the plan."

Before she could comment, his mouth came down on hers in the gentlest of kisses.

"Let me be your husband, Lexi," he whispered against her lips. "Let me hold you, feel you take me inside, and watch you touch the stars."

She heard the passion in his voice, saw the raw desire darken his eyes to navy. He pressed his lower body to hers and allowed her to feel how much he wanted to claim her as his. Her own body responded with a fevered ache.

He hadn't been forced to marry her, after all. He did want to share his life with her. Did she really want an annulment?

Ty gave her a smile that made her heart flutter. "Let me make love to you for the first time as my wife, Lexi."

Her knees began to wobble as the sound of his deep, hypnotic baritone wrapped around her. If he set his mind to it, Tyler Braden could melt the polar ice caps with his voice. She expected the emergency warning system to post flood advisories at any moment.

"You're not playing fair," she said breathlessly.

"I know," he said, brushing his lips across hers. "But I'm not feeling very fair right now."

The moment his mouth met hers, Lexi knew her body had overruled her mind in the matter. She'd hungered for Ty's touch, for his lovemaking, since that winter night in front of her fireplace in Chicago.

Ty slipped his hands beneath her sweater and pulled her closer. His palms whispered over her skin as he traced the part in her lips with his tongue, coaxing her to allow him entry. But instead of deepening the kiss, he continued to tease. His tentative touch caused a restlessness to build within her and Lexi moaned and moved against him. She wanted him to end the sweet torment, to satisfy the hunger he was creating.

"What do you want, honey?" he asked, pressing tiny kisses along her jaw, then down to her collarbones.

"I want you to kiss me, Ty," she said, her voice husky. "Really kiss me."

He raised his head to look down at her. "Is that all you want me to do?"

"No."

"What else do you want, Lexi?"

Lexi didn't have to think twice as Ty's talented hands continued to stroke her back and ribs. "I want you to make love to me, Ty."

Nine

Satisfaction flowed through Ty at her husky request. When her eyes drifted shut and her head fell back to expose the silky column of her neck, he wasted no time in taking advantage of her position. Gathering her sweater in his suddenly unsteady hands, he pulled it over her head. His normally capable fingers felt useless as he fumbled with the clasp of her bra. Once he'd released the hook and tossed it on the floor with her shirt, he was rewarded with the sight of her full breasts, the peaks tight for his touch.

He lowered his head, his tongue swirling one dark coral nipple as his thumb traced the other. When she shivered against him, he nibbled at the beaded tip before drawing it into his mouth, first chafing, then soothing. By the time he raised his head, Lexi's porcelain cheeks wore the rosy blush of desire and his own skin was coated with a fine sheen of perspiration.

The visible proof of her excitement fueled his own. He wanted to give to her as he'd never given to a woman before, but apparently Lexi had other plans. She gave him a smile filled with promise as she placed her hands on his chest and her fingers found his own sensitive flesh.

She traced the nubs with her nails. His breath rushed out in a harsh whoosh. She lowered her head to nip and tease. He stopped breathing all together.

When she raised her head to look at him, her busy fingers slid down the length of his chest and tugged at his jeans. Her seductive smile, the desire he saw darkening her eyes, caused his heart to pound and his body to strain against the denim.

Liquid fire flowed through his veins as she released the snap and slowly lowered the zipper. But when she touched the hard ridge straining at his cotton briefs, Ty felt like he just might burst into flames.

He caught her hands in his, placed them on his shoulders and reached out to slide the first button through the hole at the band of her button-fly jeans. Pure male satisfaction flowed through him as he watched her eyes glaze, heard her sharp intake of breath when his fingers dipped into the open vee to slip each button free. Releasing the last one, he slid the jeans and her silk panties down her slender legs and added them to the pile of clothes lying on the floor.

Reaching up to take Lexi's hands from his shoulders, he guided them to his waist. Lightning, keen and hot, flashed and sizzled across every nerve in his body as she lowered his jeans and briefs. By the time she'd finished the task, Ty's teeth were clenched so tightly, his jaw felt welded shut.

Her hands, as they skimmed down his hips and thighs, had almost brought him to the point of no return. But when she found him and circled his fevered flesh with her soft hands, he sucked in some much needed oxygen and stopped her delightful exploration.

"Honey, I'm not going to be able to take much more of this," he said, his mouth feeling like he could spit cotton. "It's just been too damned long."

"Then make love to me, Ty." The sound of her throaty reply bathed him with waves of heated excitement.

Ty pulled her to him and buried his face in the cloud of her golden brown hair. He shuddered at the sweet smell of honeysuckle, the feel of skin against skin and the taste of desire on her parted lips. Sweeping her into his arms, he carried her the few steps to the bed and gently placed her on top of the antique quilt.

He stared in awe at the perfection of her. "You're the most beautiful woman I've ever seen, Lexi. And you're mine. My wife. The mother of my son."

Joining her on the bed, Ty took her into his arms and kissed her with all the awe and wonder of a man who realized what a precious gift he'd been given.

She threaded her slender fingers in his hair and the fire inside him began to build even hotter. Exploring, reacquainting himself with her body, he stroked her dewy softness. Her complete readiness for him, the arching of her hips as she met each caress, caused the flames to flare out of control.

Desire, hot and urgent, thrummed through his veins, but Ty somehow managed to find the strength to leave her for a moment. The preventive measure in place, he gathered her to him, covered her body with his and nudged her knees apart. Their gazes met and locked as he slowly eased himself inside.

He heard her breath catch, saw the rapture reflected in her expressive eyes as he filled her completely. There was so much he wanted to tell her. So many things he needed to say. But with his body held intimately inside hers, and with passion illuminating her beautiful face, words were simply impossible.

"Lexi," was all he could get out as he lowered his mouth to hers.

The sweet taste of desire on her perfect lips, the feel of her softness surrounding him, unleashed the taut energy he'd fought to control. Spirals of hunger and need wrapped around them as in perfect unison they yielded to the ultimate dance of love. Together they reached for the stars and they both cried out at the beauty of it when their souls found heaven awaiting in one brilliant burst of heat and light.

His breathing slowly returned to normal and Ty eased himself to her side. He wrapped his arms around her and she murmured his name a moment before falling asleep. Being up most of the night had taken its toll on both of them. His last thought before sleep overtook him was how good it felt to have her back in his arms.

"Ty, wake up," Lexi said gently shaking his shoulder. "You're having a nightmare."

Ty sat up with his back to her. Coated with cold sweat, his body trembled and his heart pounded as if it were going to leap from his chest. Taking deep breaths, he tried to regain his composure before he faced her.

"What were you dreaming about?" she asked, clearly concerned. "It must have been terrible."

He jerked around to face her. "Did I say anything?"

She looked startled at his harsh tone. "Yes. But I couldn't understand what it was. You were pretty incoherent."

Ty ran a hand over his face and tried to rub the images from his mind.

"It was just a dream, Ty." She placed her hand on his shoulder. "Do you want to tell me about it?"

"No!" Without another word, he left the bed and stalked into the bathroom.

Bracing his hands on the bathroom sink, he bowed his head and took several deep breaths. When he finally felt steady enough to glance at the mirror, he barely recognized the haggard man staring back at him.

He'd never before thought of himself as a coward. Hell, he'd stared death in the face more times than he cared to count in the course of treating young gang members and deranged addicts. But staring down the barrel of a Saturday night special or watching the polished, steel point of a switchblade slash the air hadn't caused him a fraction of the terror that twisted at his gut now.

If he told Lexi what happened that snowy evening almost a year ago—the night they'd made love—why he'd been desperate to be held, and why he'd recently had to leave Chicago, he might lose her and their son for good. He gritted his teeth against the thought of her reaction. He couldn't bear to watch condemnation glaze her eyes.

Or worse yet, fear. He'd rather die than to have her be afraid of him.

But maintaining his silence wasn't the answer either. By his response when she asked him to talk about the dream, she had to know he was hiding something.

Ty shut his eyes against the battle raging within. Either way, he ran the risk of losing her.

When she left Chicago almost a year ago, it had taken him several months to stop looking for her each time he stepped into the elevator, to keep from laying in bed each night wondering what would have happened if she'd stayed in the city. But this time he knew for certain it wouldn't be as simple as that. If she sent him away, this time he doubted he'd survive.

"Lexi, you haven't heard a word I've said," Freddie complained, removing a sheet from the clothesline.

"I'm sorry." Lexi gave her sister-in-law an apologetic smile. "I guess I'm a little tired."

"Well, I would hope so." Freddie grinned. "After all, you are a newlywed."

Tears threatened as Lexi glanced down at her son snuggled close to her breast. She'd taken the baby for a walk and found herself at Jeff and Freddie's house. She knew deep down it wasn't by accident that her walk had her visiting her sister-in-law. Lexi needed someone to talk to and Freddie had been her confidante since they'd been seated next to each other in Miss Barnes's first-grade class at Dixie Ridge Grade School.

But from the moment Lexi arrived, Freddie had chattered a mile a minute about what a lovely family the three of them made. And with each comment, Lexi felt her heart break just a little more.

She bit her lower lip to keep it from trembling. "My fatigue isn't from what you think," she finally said.

Freddie folded the sheet, then placed it in a large wicker basket, her bright smile fading. "Things aren't goin' well?"

"Not really."

Freddie gave her a measuring look before heading toward the house. "Why don't you put Matthew down for a nap in the spare bedroom, while I make a pot of coffee?"

Following her sister-in-law into the house, Lexi made sure Matthew was asleep before joining Freddie at the kitchen table.

"So, what's wrong?" Freddie asked, placing a steamy cup of coffee in front of Lexi. "You look like your favorite bird dog died."

Lexi wiped at a lone tear making a trail down her cheek. "I'm afraid it's not going to work, Freddie."

Freddie reached out to place her hand on Lexi's arm. "I'm sure in time things will work out."

"You don't understand." Lexi shook her head as she stared down at the cup clutched tightly between her palms. "It's not anything as simple as adjusting to him leaving his socks on the bathroom floor or the cap off the toothpaste. Ty is hiding something that's tearing him apart, but he won't let me help." Her gaze met Freddie's. "A few days ago he had this horrible nightmare, and I could tell he was reliving something terrible. But when I tried to get him to talk to me, he flat-out refused."

Freddie looked thoughtful. "Did you stop to think it might be too painful for him to talk about?"

"That's possible," Lexi conceded. "He did tell me about his family, so he is opening up."

"Give him a little more time," Freddie suggested. "You've only been married a few days. Some things take longer to share. You can't expect him to just unload everything all at once." She gave Lexi a wink. "I have faith in you, girl. You'll bring him around."

Lexi took a deep breath. "I hope you're right."

"I know I am." Freddie checked her watch. "Granny's garters! Jeff will be home in an hour and I haven't even thought about what to fix for supper."

When she rose from her chair, the color drained from Freddie's face and she gripped the table to keep from falling.

Lexi jumped to her feet and put her arm around her sister-in-law's shoulders. "What's wrong?"

"I'm okay." Freddie grinned sheepishly. "I've just got to learn not to move so fast, that's all."

"Are you sure you're all right?" Lexi asked, not at all convinced. Freddie's face was still a pasty white and her breathing seemed labored.

"I couldn't be better," Freddie assured a moment before her eyes fluttered shut and she completely lost her battle with consciousness.

Lexi rose from the chair when she heard Jeff's truck come to a sliding halt in front of the house. It didn't surprise her in the least that her brother had made the forty-minute drive from Gatlinburg in a little over twenty. When she'd called his cabinet shop and explained the situation, she'd immediately found herself talking to an open line.

The front door crashed open with a resounding thud as Jeff's long strides carried him well into the room. "Where's Freddie?" he demanded.

"In the bedroom," Lexi said. She caught hold of his arm when he started toward the hall. "Ty's with her now."

Jeff glanced down at the hand Lexi placed on his forearm, then looked at her as if seeing her for the first time. He took a deep shuddering breath before he finally asked, "What happened?"

Lexi explained what had taken place, then added, "She refused to go to the clinic, so I called Ty."

Jeff's tight nod was almost imperceptible. "How long has he been in there with her?"

She checked the clock on the mantle. "About ten minutes. It shouldn't be much longer."

"I can't understand it. She's always been healthy as a…" Jeff's voice trailed off at the sound of a door opening and two people coming down the hall.

When they walked into the living room, Ty was smiling and Freddie looked absolutely radiant.

At his wife's side in a heartbeat, Jeff put his arm around her shoulders for support. "What happened, sweetheart? Are you all right?"

Lexi watched Freddie glance at Ty and grin before she wrapped her arms around Jeff's waist. "I couldn't be better, Love Dumplin'. I just got a little woozy, that's all."

Jeff's cheeks turned red. "I asked you not to call me that in front of people," he muttered. He hugged his wife close and turned to Ty. "Why did she faint?"

Ty grinned. "I think I'll let your wife tell you."

"Well, somebody better tell me," Jeff said, clearly losing patience. "And damned quick."

Freddie giggled. "Don't get your shorts in a bunch, big guy. Ty said feelin' faint sometimes happens to pregnant ladies."

The silence that accompanied Freddie's announcement lasted only a split second before Jeff swept his petite wife into his arms and let out a whoop that could have raised the dead. "We're gonna have a baby."

"That's wonderful," Lexi exclaimed, relieved that nothing was seriously wrong.

She glanced at Ty and felt a twinge of regret. When she'd found out Matthew was on the way, she hadn't been able to make such a joyous announcement. She'd gone home in a state of shock to an empty house and tried to make plans for her future as a single mother.

Ty's intense blue gaze met hers from across the room and they stared at each other for several long moments. She could see the regret, and knew he was thinking of what he'd missed during her pregnancy with Matthew.

She wanted more than anything for their marriage to work. Maybe Freddie was right. Maybe if she gave him more time, he'd open up, allow her to help, and they could start building a future together.

"Thanks for comin' here to the house," Jeff said, interrupting her thoughts. He reached out to shake Ty's hand. "Freddie wouldn't go inside the clinic unless it was a matter of life and death."

Ty shrugged. "No problem. I'd just seen my last patient for the day when Lexi called."

"I'm so happy for both of you," Lexi said, smiling. "You've waited a long time for this."

"We sure have," Jeff said. He tucked Freddie

close to his side and grinned down at her. "We've got some celebratin' to do, sweetheart."

Lexi watched her brother gaze lovingly at his wife. She had a good idea what Jeff had planned for the evening and it certainly didn't include her and Ty.

An ache settled around her heart. In time, maybe Ty could learn to love her the way Jeff loved Freddie. He'd said he wanted to give their marriage a chance, to work at being a whole family. Wasn't that what she wanted too? He had shared his illegitimacy with her—something that had been very difficult for him. It wasn't everything, but it was a start. In time, maybe he could learn to love and trust her with whatever haunted him. But she'd never know if she didn't try.

"It's almost time for Matthew's dinner, isn't it, Lexi?" Ty asked, winking.

She smiled. "As a matter of fact, I think it is."

When she, Ty and the baby left Jeff's and Freddie's house, Lexi doubted that either one of the pair even noticed.

"There must have been something to Granny Applegate's prediction last month," Ty said steering the SUV onto the road.

"Which one was that?" Lexi asked.

He laughed. "The one about the moon being right for women becoming pregnant. Freddie's is the third pregnancy I've diagnosed today."

"A baby boom on Piney Knob."

"Looks like it," he agreed.

They fell into an uneasy silence as they drove up the lane to the cabin.

He hated the strained atmosphere between them, the caution. He knew he was only postponing the inevitable. There were things that, as his wife, Lexi had a right to know.

When he parked the truck in front of the house, Lexi surprised him by getting out of the back seat and getting into the bucket seat on the passenger side. Turning to face him, she reached out to hug him.

''Honey—''

''It doesn't matter right now, Ty. We'll take things one step at a time. I'll be here to listen when you're ready.''

Incapable of finding the right words to express how he felt at her gentle reassurance, he kissed her.

Heat shot through him when her lips met his. Her fingers threaded through the hair at the base of his neck and urged him closer. Allowing her to take control of the kiss, he felt a jolt of desire as strong as an electric current course through him. She stroked his lips with her tongue, then nipped at them with her teeth. Never in his wildest dreams could he think of anything more provocative than Lexi taking the role of seductress.

The fire she was building inside him with her tentative exploration heightened his senses and caused his body to tighten to an almost painful state. When she urged him to open for her, he groaned at the sweet taste of her, the tantalizing smell of honeysuckle as it seductively wrapped around him.

His mind and body zeroing in on one thought, it took him several seconds to realize a truck horn blared from somewhere behind them. Breaking the kiss, he glanced in the rearview mirror to see Carl Morgan climb down from the cab of his truck and start toward them.

"Damn!" He reached for the door handle. "Don't these people have lives of their own?"

"I used to think so," Lexi said. She got out of the truck, then opening the rear door, released the catch on the baby's protective carrier. "I'll take Matthew inside, while you see what Carl wants."

Ty cursed vehemently, got out of the Blazer and slammed the door. How the hell did these people ever expect a newly married couple to find happiness when they wouldn't leave them alone?

"What can I do for you, Carl?" he asked impatiently.

Not at all put off by Ty's abrupt tone, Carl grinned. "Sorry 'bout hornin' in on your business there, Doc. I promise I'll let you get back to Lexi in just a few minutes. But I wanted to stop by and bring you somethin' to show how much I appreciate all you did for Liddy and the baby the other night."

Ty heaved a sigh. He felt like a heel. "It's not necessary, Carl."

"Yes, it is," the big man insisted. He motioned for Ty to follow him. Walking to the back of his truck he pointed to the bed. "I promised you I'd make sure you didn't regret comin' to Dixie Ridge and I never go back on my word."

Ty started to say he wouldn't regret coming to the mountains if everyone would just leave him and Lexi alone. Instead, he found himself counting to ten as he tried to regain some of his usual patience.

"Carl, I was just doing what I came here to do. You don't have to—"

The words died in Ty's throat when he saw what Carl had in mind. There in the middle of the truck bed, a big red bow tied around its neck, a black-and-white pig the size of a cocker spaniel sat as regal as any monarch.

"This here's Dempsey," Carl said, grinning. "He's a registered Hampshire."

"Dempsey?"

"Yeah, but don't blame me for callin' him that. The boys name 'em as soon as they're born." Carl shrugged. "Anyway, Dempsey is yours now."

"Mine?" Ty shook his head. He didn't want to insult the man, but he needed a pig about as much as the North Pole needed ice cubes. "I appreciate the gesture, but I can't accept him, Carl. I'll be going back to the city in a few months. Besides, I don't know the first thing about taking care of a pig. I don't even know what they eat."

"Pigs are easy to get the hang of," Carl said, lowering the tailgate. He unloaded a huge pail and carried it to the porch. "And don't worry none about what to feed him. I'll keep you supplied with plenty of my special recipe." He patted the top of the bucket with his big, beefy hand. "Just give him a scoop of this a couple of times a day and he'll be fine."

"Carl, I can't let you do this," Ty insisted. "I told you I'll be going back to Chicago."

The man just grinned, tied a rope around Dempsey's neck for a leash, then placed the pig in Ty's arms. He slammed the tailgate shut and headed for the driver's side door. "Welcome to Piney Knob, Doc."

"I don't have a place to keep him," Ty tried, feeling desperate. What the hell was he going to do with a pig?

"He'll be fine right back there," Carl said, pointing to the shed behind the cabin. Having solved that problem, the man crawled into the cab, turned the truck around and waved as he drove out of sight.

Dempsey grunted and squirmed, then emitted a large burp.

Ty glanced down at the small pig tucked in his arms. He felt like he'd entered the Twilight Zone for the second time in a week.

Five minutes ago he was well on his way to making love to his wife. Now he stood, holding a squinty-eyed little pig that appeared to have digestive problems.

He cursed and set Dempsey on his feet. Ty watched the pig's wobbly trot as he led the animal to the shed. Great! Dempsey probably had inner ear trouble to go along with his gassy stomach.

Ty decided he'd worry later about a remedy for the little porker's problem. He wanted to get back to Lexi before someone else showed up to ruin what had started out to be a promising evening with his wife.

Ten

Lexi finished nursing Matthew, then placed her sleeping son in the cradle. She wondered what was taking Ty so long. She hoped he wasn't being called away on another emergency.

They needed time together. Time to talk. Time to start building a foundation of trust between them.

She walked into the great room just as Ty entered the house. "What did Carl want?"

Ty rolled his eyes and shook his head. "I can't believe it. We are now the proud owners of a black and white pig named Dempsey."

"Carl gave you one of his registered Hampshires?" she asked incredulously. "He must really be grateful. Those animals are quite valuable."

"Only if you make a movie about him talking to sheep," Ty muttered.

She shook her head. "Wrong breed of pig."

"Whatever."

Lexi might have laughed had it not been for Ty's exasperated expression. "What did you do with him?"

"I put him in the shed." He wrinkled his nose and shook his head in disgust. "Along with a really foul-smelling bucket of pig food."

That did it. She couldn't contain her laughter any longer. "You don't want to own a pig?"

"No." He crossed the room and took her into his arms. Lowering his head, he brushed her lips with his. "And I don't want to think about it now."

Ty's kiss made her pulse race and her stomach flutter. She didn't want to think about a pig named Dempsey either.

"Is Matthew asleep?" he asked when he raised his head. His blue eyes had darkened with desire, and the hunger she saw there took her breath away.

"Yes."

She watched the pulse at the base of his throat quicken and she leaned forward to kiss it. The slight movement against her lips sent tingles over every nerve in her body.

"He should sleep for a couple of hours," she offered.

Ty traced his finger along her cheek as he stared down at her. "I'm going to take a shower. I'll only be a few minutes."

Lexi nodded and watched Ty walk down the hall. She waited patiently until he closed the bathroom door, then followed him. When she heard the water running, she grinned. He hadn't asked her to join him, but some things were more provocative when done on impulse.

Her breath caught when she entered the bathroom and watched Ty's masculine form silhouetted through the frosty glass of the shower doors.

She quickly shed her clothes, opened the door and stepped inside. "I'll wash your back, if you wash mine."

"What took you so long?" he asked, his voice low and suggestive as he reached for her.

Ty's arms closed around her to pull her forward. If she could remember what he'd asked, she might have answered. But the feel of his hard, wet maleness pressed to her sent ribbons of desire threading their way through every part of her, and she forgot her own name, let alone anything she'd been about to say.

His hands ran the length of her back to the curve of her bottom, then up her sides to the swell of her breasts. He supported the heaviness he'd created there as he lowered his lips to sip the water droplets from her skin. Her body tingled. He took one beaded tip into his mouth, then the other to tease them with his strong teeth and slightly rough tongue. When he raised his head, he kissed her like she'd never been kissed before, and the taste of his passion left her weak and wanting.

Lexi ran her hands over his shoulders, his wide chest, his flanks. She wanted to give to him as he gave to her. When she touched him, her fingers closed around his length and she was rewarded with his groan of pleasure as she tested his strength, soothed him with her palm.

He caught her hands in his and placed them on his shoulders as he knelt before her. "You're beautiful," he said, his lips skimming her satin skin.

His hands slid over her hips to her inner thighs and

when he found her, she felt as if she might go up in flames. Heat threatened to consume her as Ty's finger dipped inside to tease, caress, stroke. He treated her to the same sweet torture she'd subjected him to only moments before.

When she thought she'd surely die from the pleasure of his touch, he rose to his feet and lifted her to him. Their gazes locked as Lexi circled his shoulders with her arms and wrapped her legs around him. Without a word, he braced himself against the shower wall and slid himself inside her.

Lexi gasped at the intense pleasure of being filled by him. She closed her eyes and her head fell back as she arched against him, taking all he had to give, trying to absorb his body with hers.

Ty moved and the coil of need in her belly tightened, the exquisite pleasure almost more than she could bear. With each powerful stroke the pressure increased and she found herself clinging to the moment, responding in ways she'd never before experienced. He must have sensed her readiness, her fierce need of fulfillment because he brought his hands down to cup her bottom, holding her more tightly to him as he increased the rhythm.

Just when she thought she could take no more, spirals of heat and light raced through her and Lexi clung to Ty as her body shattered into a million pieces. She felt him stiffen a moment before he joined her in the all-consuming pleasure, releasing his essence deep inside her.

Lexi slowly drifted back to earth as Ty slid them to a sitting position on the floor of the shower. Exhausted, water cascading over both of them, she lowered her forehead to his shoulder.

"It's never been like that," she whispered.

Ty shook his head as he stroked her wet hair. "For me, either."

She leaned back to look at him. "I think I'm falling in love with you."

It hurt that he wasn't returning her confession of love, but his eyes darkened to navy a moment before he lowered his mouth to hers. He kissed her with a tenderness that stole her breath and chased away all thought.

When the kiss ended, he reached up to turn off the water. "Let's find a more comfortable place to continue this, honey."

Nodding, Lexi rose to her feet, opened the door and reached for one of the thick towels on the rack beside the shower. She blotted the water from Ty's wide chest and shoulders, but when she started to dry his legs, her breath caught and her stomach fluttered at the sight of his rapidly changing body.

"You seem to have a recurring problem, Dr. Braden."

"Looks like it." He grinned suggestively. "Want to help me find the cure?"

"Well, I don't have any formal medical training," Lexi said, returning his smile.

He took her hand in his and led her into the bedroom. Taking her into his arms, he whispered close to her ear, "Sometimes there's no better way to learn than hands-on training."

And, as his hands once again began to work their magic, Lexi decided she had to agree.

"It appears you have your days and nights mixed up," Ty said, picking up his smiling son.

He glanced over at the bed to see if Matthew's cooing had awakened Lexi. She slept peacefully.

Ty cradled the baby to him and quietly walked down the hall. "We don't want to disturb Mommy. She's really tired."

Walking into the living room, he turned on a lamp, then settled himself and the baby in the rocking chair. "I want to thank you for being a good boy and taking such a long nap this evening," Ty said, kissing the baby's soft cheek. "It gave Daddy a chance to spend some time with Mommy."

Matthew gave him a toothless baby smile and gurgled.

Ty chuckled. "You understand, don't you, little man?"

The baby's tiny hand bumped against Ty's ring finger and curled around it in a surprisingly strong grip.

Ty gazed down at his son's hand so close to the gold ring circling his finger. He'd never allowed himself to think of what it would be like to be a husband and father. Never thought he'd feel the kind of love he experienced at this moment. He wanted it to last forever.

Being away from the stress and tremendous pressure he'd been under for the last several years, he'd had time to think. He wasn't sure what the future held, but he knew for certain he wouldn't be going back to the E.R. when he returned to Chicago. Treating the patients of Dixie Ridge, he'd discovered he liked the more relaxed pace of private practice.

Setting up an office in a quiet suburb would be something to consider. Then maybe Lexi would be receptive to going back with him.

He glanced at the hall, then leaned his head back

and closed his eyes. Before that happened, Lexi deserved to know about the man she'd married. The man who'd fathered her child.

Time was running out. Dr. Fletcher would be returning to resume his practice at the Dixie Ridge Health Clinic in a few months and Ty would be leaving. If Lexi and Matthew went back to Chicago with him, she'd learn all too soon about the sins of the man she'd married.

And it scared the hell out of him.

"Honey, could you come here?" Ty called from outside.

Concerned by the worry she detected in his voice, Lexi shifted Matthew to her shoulder and hurried out onto the porch. She found Ty standing in the yard with Dempsey.

"What's the problem?"

"Call Jeff and tell him I won't be going fishing with him today."

"Why not?"

Ty glanced down at the pig and frowned. "Something's wrong with Dempsey."

She watched the little pig stagger closer to Ty. "What makes you think that?" she asked, barely able to keep a straight face.

The little pig chose that moment to sit down and lean his head against Ty's leg.

"I fed him about an hour ago and now he can barely stand up." He reached down to give Dempsey a sympathetic pat on the head. "I'd better take the poor thing to a vet."

Dempsey emitted a loud burp, grunted contentedly and gave Lexi a glassy-eyed stare.

She tried not to laugh, but it was no use. She knew exactly what Dempsey's problem was. "Ty, you don't have anything to worry about. There's nothing wrong with that pig that time won't take care of."

He looked skeptical. "Are you sure? From the smell of that stuff Carl gave me to feed him, I think he might have food poisoning."

When Dempsey lay down on his side and immediately started snoring, Lexi laughed so hard, tears filled her eyes.

Ty glanced down at Dempsey again, then gave her a long, measuring look. "Why do I get the idea you know something I don't? This pig isn't sick, is he?"

She shook her head as she came to stand next to him. "How much of that feed did you give him?"

"Carl said to feed him one scoop twice a day." Ty frowned. "But he still seemed hungry so I gave him another scoop."

Lexi nodded. "That's what I thought. Carl doesn't raise hogs for his main source of income, although they do contribute to it. He keeps them to get rid of the by-product created by his real line of work."

Ty raised one dark brown. "And that would be?"

Smiling, she kissed his cheek. "Carl runs one of the most productive stills on Piney Knob."

"He makes moonshine?"

Lexi laughed at his incredulous expression. "Yes, and it's a well-known fact that pigs love the taste of fermented corn. That's why Carl keeps them."

Understanding crossed Ty's handsome face. "They dispose of the grain once it's been used to make the liquor. When I gave Dempsey extra, it was more than he's used to."

Grinning, she nodded. "You exceeded Dempsey's tolerance level."

Ty looked thoroughly disgusted. "Bottom line, I got Dempsey drunk."

"Yes, Dr. Braden." Lexi laughed. "You're guilty of contributing to the delinquency of a pig."

"I'm not sure this is such a good idea," Ty said, following Jeff through the woods. "I know even less about fishing than I do about feeding pigs."

Jeff laughed. "Don't worry about that pig. He'll sleep it off. Besides, goin' fishin' is just an excuse."

"For what?" Ty ducked and barely avoided being slapped across the face by the low-hanging branch Jeff had shoved aside. "You want to enlighten me on the real reason we're out here in the woods, risking life and limb?"

"I've got some things I want to ask you about Freddie's condition," Jeff called over his shoulder, continuing up the path. "I don't want Freddie or Lexi gettin' wind of how little I know about pregnant ladies. They'd never let me live it down."

"There's no big mystery," Ty said, trying to keep up with Jeff and dodge the sharp briars snatching at his clothes.

"That's easy for you to say," Jeff retorted. "You've been to school for stuff like this."

"What is it you want to know?" Ty asked, stopping to unsnag his sleeve from a briar.

"Am I gonna be gettin' up in the middle of the night to drive over to Gatlinburg for stuff like pickles and ice cream or some other ungodly combination of food?"

Ty chuckled. "There are no guarantees. Some

women do crave strange things. But it's not set in stone that Freddie will be one of them. She might not have any cravings at all.''

"That makes me feel a little better," Jeff grumbled. He shuddered visibly. "I don't much cotton to the idea of havin' to watch her eat that stuff.''

They walked on in silence for several yards, before Ty asked, "Was there anything else you wanted to know?''

Jeff stopped abruptly and turned to face him. "Yes, there is.''

From the expression on the man's face, Ty could tell Jeff wanted to discuss more important matters than Freddie's future eating habits.

"Have you ever considered doin' home deliveries?" Jeff asked, point-blank. "I wouldn't be askin', but we both know how Freddie feels about goin' inside the clinic.''

"No, I've never considered it. But it's a moot point anyway.'' Ty rubbed at the tension building at the base of his neck. Lately, every time he thought of going back to the city, his muscles tensed and his gut twisted. "I'll be going back to Chicago well before Freddie gives birth. Besides, I thought Freddie preferred Granny Applegate.''

"Maybe she does. But I don't.'' His expression determined, Jeff explained, "Don't get me wrong. Granny is a real fine woman, but she's been talkin' lately about retirin'. I doubt she'll even be midwifin' when Freddie needs her.''

"She mentioned something about that at the wedding reception,'' Ty said, nodding.

Jeff shrugged. "I just want the best for my wife

and baby. I'd feel better about a doctor takin' care of Freddie when her time comes."

Ty fully understood Jeff's concerns. "I don't blame you. Talk to Dr. Fletcher when he returns. Maybe you can make some kind of arrangement with him."

Jeff nodded. "I guess I can try."

Ty met his brother-in-law's concerned gaze. "I'm making no promises, but I'll talk to Fletcher and ask him to give it serious consideration."

Jeff grinned. "That'd be great. Thanks."

They started back up the path, but a sharp, loud crack stopped them both in their tracks.

Ty heard a dull thud as something hit the tree beside him. "What the hell was that?" he asked, brushing chips of bark from his hair.

"Get down!" Jeff shouted, turning to grab Ty by the arm.

No sooner had Jeff taken hold of his arm than a second crack split the air and Ty felt the ground rush up to meet him. The outside of his upper left arm felt as if it had been set on fire and he automatically reached up to soothe the burning. He must have hit it on something when Jeff pulled him down, he decided, rubbing the area.

"You okay?" Jeff asked.

"Yes. What's going on?"

Jeff looked around the now eerily silent woods. "In case you hadn't noticed, we're being shot at."

"Who would—"

"I'm not sure," Jeff interrupted. "But we need to get out of here."

Ty put his left hand down to push himself to his knees, but white-hot pain suddenly shot up his arm and he glanced at the spot to see his shirt was torn.

Shock and revulsion coursed through him at the surreal sight of his own blood rapidly soaking the fabric. Throughout his years in an inner-city hospital emergency room, he'd faced all kinds of threats, but never once had he actually been injured.

"Let's get back to the truck," Jeff said, rising to his feet. He began gathering their fishing rods and tackle box. "Whoever fired that gun must have cleared out, and I think we'd better do the same before he comes back with some buddies."

Ty put his right hand over the wound and attempted to regain his footing, but slightly off balance, he sank back to his knees. "You're going to have to help me get up," he said through clenched teeth. "I've been shot."

Jeff dropped the fishing gear and knelt beside him. "Damn! How bad is it?"

"There isn't enough blood for it to have severed an artery," Ty said. "I think it's just a flesh wound. But it burns like hell."

"Let me take a look," Jeff said.

Ty removed his hand for Jeff to peel back the torn edges of his shirtsleeve. The bullet had cut a path across the outside of Ty's upper arm, but the damage seemed minimal.

"It's going to take a few stitches to close, but otherwise it isn't bad," Ty said, feeling somewhat detached as his physician's eyes assessed the wound.

At that moment, the sound of brush being pushed aside and heavy footsteps caused them to look up. Carl Morgan, rifle in hand, was bearing down on them like a charging bull.

"Aw hell, Doc, I didn't know it was you and Jeff," he said, dropping to his knees beside Ty. "I wasn't meanin' to hit anybody. I was just tryin' to warn y'all away from—''

''You thought we were the authorities comin' to bust up your still, didn't you?'' Jeff accused, removing his handkerchief from his hip pocket and winding it around Ty's arm.

Carl's shoulders drooped. ''Yeah. They've been lookin' for my boiler for the past six months,'' he admitted. ''But I've always stayed one step ahead of 'em. This bein' my last batch and all, I just wanted to get it jugged and out of here before I busted up the cooker.''

''You're going to stop making moonshine?'' Ty asked.

Carl nodded. ''I promised Liddy that if we ever had a baby girl, I'd quit runnin' shine and go to raisin' hogs full-time.''

''Why does havin' a daughter make a difference?'' Jeff asked, securing the makeshift bandage on Ty's arm.

''Little girls are special,'' Carl said simply. A wondrous expression crossed his face as he hooked his thumbs in the straps of his overalls and explained. ''I don't want to take a chance of bein' caught makin' white lightnin' and get myself thrown in jail. I don't want little Carly ashamed of her daddy.'' His expression turned to one of pure misery when he glanced down at Ty's arm. ''Now this had to happen. You're gonna have to report this, ain't you, Doc?''

Ty stared off into the distance as he pondered what he would do. In Chicago, he'd viewed things as black and white. Right and wrong. Legal and illegal. And he wouldn't have thought twice about turning Carl in to the authorities.

But here in the mountains, it was a different story. Since being here in Dixie Ridge, Ty had learned to be flexible, to take into account the gray areas as well as the black and white of a situation.

Carl wasn't just a nameless face in the crowd. He was a friend. A neighbor. A loving husband and father. A man who deserved a chance to mend his ways.

Ty had no idea why a daughter's opinion meant more than a son's, but he wasn't going to question Carl's logic. The fact that the man was going to quit the illegal activity was all that mattered.

"As a doctor, I'm supposed to report any kind of gunshot wound," Ty admitted. "But I think I can overlook this, *if* you keep your word and cease making moonshine."

Carl brightened. "You have my word. I won't make another drop." Glancing at the handkerchief wrapped around Ty's arm, blood already staining the pristine white, his expression turned dark once again. "Damn! Lexi's gonna have my hide for shootin' you."

"It wasn't your fault," Ty said, shrugging.

Jeff and Carl gave him a look that stated quite clearly they both thought he'd lost his mind.

Ty grinned. "I have no idea who fired the gun or why."

Jeff chuckled as he caught on to Ty's meaning. "I don't either."

His voice suspiciously hoarse, Carl got to his feet. "I owe you both. I'll see that you don't regret it."

Ty quickly shook his head. "No more pigs, Carl. Just get rid of that still and we'll call it even."

"Thanks, Doc," Carl said, reaching out to shake Ty's hand. "I won't forget this."

"I'll take Ty down to the clinic so Martha can clean and bandage his arm," Jeff said, helping Ty to his feet. "Carl, you get your 'shine jugged, then bust up that boiler."

"I surely will," Carl said a moment before he picked up his rifle and disappeared back into the dense woods.

"We'll stop by the cabin and get Lexi on our way down to Dixie Ridge," Jeff stated, gathering their fishing gear.

Ty shook his head. "No. She's probably busy with the baby. Besides, it's no big deal."

Jeff stopped to give him a knowing grin. "You don't know much about women, do you?"

"I know enough," Ty said as they started back down Piney Knob.

"No, you don't," Jeff retorted. "Wives make a big deal out of everything."

"Lexi won't. She's levelheaded and I'm sure she'll understand."

Jeff's laugh echoed through the woods. "I hope you remember that while she's readin' you the riot act."

Lexi stopped doing sit-ups to stare at her sister-in-law. "Mary Ann Simmons and Jake Sanders are finally getting married?"

"That's what Miss Eunice was tellin' me when I stopped by to see about orderin' some maternity clothes." Her hazel eyes dancing merrily, Freddie plopped down on the exercise mat beside Lexi. "And you'll never guess where they've decided to get hitched."

"Where?"

"You remember how Mary Ann always tried to copy everything you did when we were in school?" Freddie asked.

Lexi sat up to blot perspiration from her face with a soft towel. "Don't tell me—"

Laughing, Freddie nodded. "She's insistin' she wants a weddin' just like yours. She's asked Miss Eunice if it would be all right for them to be married in the dress shop and use the weddin' display, just like you and Ty."

"Oh, good grief!" When she finally stopped laughing, Lexi shook her head. "I can't believe it. I figured Mary Ann would still be chasing Jake around Dixie Ridge when they were both too old to run."

Freddie grinned. "Well, she might have been, if the moon hadn't been right."

Lexi's mouth fell open. "She's pregnant?"

"Yep. And Jake's struttin' around like a peacock with his tail fanned. I stopped by the Blue Bird after I left the dress shop, and he was grinnin' from ear to ear."

"Ty mentioned that he'd diagnosed several maternity cases lately," Lexi said thoughtfully. "I wonder who else is pregnant."

Freddie shrugged. "I don't know. But rumor has it that Granny Applegate has decided to quit deliverin' babies."

"Oh, Freddie," Lexi said, her tone sympathetic. "What will you do?"

"Jeff is talkin' to Ty right now about startin' home deliveries." Freddie smiled. "He told me he wants the best for me and the baby." Her eyes filled with tears. "Isn't that just the sweetest thing?"

Lexi didn't have the heart to remind her sister-in-law of Ty's imminent departure when Doc Fletcher returned. She hadn't wanted to think about it herself.

Ty would go back to Chicago and she'd stay here to raise Matthew in the unhurried pace of the mountains. She'd like nothing more than to give her marriage to Ty a chance, but no matter how much she loved him, it didn't change the fact that he obviously didn't return her feelings.

Biting her lower lip to keep it from trembling, she reached out to hug Freddie. "It doesn't surprise me in the least that Jeff's talking to Ty about home delivery. That brother of mine loves you with all his heart and soul."

And I wish with all my heart that Ty felt the same way about me.

When the phone rang, Lexi groaned and slowly rose to her feet. "Now where on earth did I put that cordless phone?" she asked, sniffing back tears as she searched the end tables.

"Ours always manages to slip down between the couch cushions," Freddie said, joining the search.

Just as Lexi found the phone, the answering machine picked up.

"Lexi, get down here as soon as you can." Martha's worried voice filtered into the room. "Doc's been hurt. Jeff just brought him into the clinic."

Eleven

"**W**here's Ty?" Lexi demanded when she found her brother in the clinic's small reception area.

Jeff lounged in one of the chairs, his long legs stretched out in front of him, ankles crossed. He didn't look like he had a care in the world.

"Martha's got him back there in one of the exam rooms, stitchin' up his arm," he said, then had the audacity to yawn.

Trying to get the details from her brother about what had taken place was proving as difficult as pulling a hen's teeth. Never in her entire life had Lexi wanted to hit someone as much as she wanted to punch Jeff at that moment. She might have too, had she not been holding Matthew.

"Jeff Hatfield, you'd better answer your sister," Freddie said, stepping around Lexi. "And you'd better do it right now."

At the sight of his wife standing inside the walls of the clinic, Jeff was on his feet in a split second, his mouth agape. "Freddie, sweetheart, what the hell are you doing in here?"

Had it not been for the gravity of the situation, Lexi might have laughed at the startled expression on her brother's face. But at the moment her main concern was Ty.

"What happened?" she asked impatiently. "When Martha called all she said was that Ty had been hurt."

Jeff shifted from one foot to the other. "I should have known Martha wouldn't let her shirttail hit her backside until she called and got you all riled up."

"Dammit, Jeff, I'm beginnin' to lose patience with you," Freddie warned, taking the baby from Lexi.

"Uh, well, he got shot," Jeff finally stammered.

Tears filled Lexi's eyes and she began to shake uncontrollably. "Oh, dear Lord!"

"It's okay, Sis." Jeff folded her into his arms. "It's just a flesh wound. He's okay."

"I've got to see for myself," Lexi said. Pulling away, she turned to Freddie. "Could you—"

"Don't worry about Matthew," Freddie said, shifting the baby to her shoulder. "We'll take care of him. You go check on Ty."

Nodding, Lexi hurried down the hall. When she heard voices behind one of the exam room doors, she didn't think twice about walking right in.

"I figured it was about time for you to get here," Martha said. She tied and clipped a suture, then glanced at the clock on the wall. "Tied the record coming down Piney Knob, too. Freddie must have been drivin'."

Ty sat shirtless on the exam table, a scowl crossing his handsome face. "I told Jeff not to call."

"He didn't," Lexi said, her gaze running over every inch of her husband. Other than the nasty-looking wound Martha attended to on his upper left arm, Ty looked to be all right.

"I didn't want you— Ouch! Dammit, Martha, will you take it easy?"

Lexi felt her heart shatter into a million pieces, along with her hopes of making their marriage work. He didn't have to finish what he'd started to say. It was perfectly clear Ty didn't want her with him.

Tears threatened, but she somehow found the strength to force them back. "I thought you might need me with you," she stated, thankful that her voice remained steady despite the huge lump clogging her throat. "Apparently I was wrong. Have Jeff give you a ride home."

"Lexi, I didn't mean—"

But Ty found himself talking to an empty doorway. He cursed under his breath. He'd tried to tell her he hadn't wanted to worry her.

"I'm the one who called," Martha admitted, reaching for a roll of gauze. She began wrapping it around his arm. "And if somethin' like this happens in the future, you can bet your bottom dollar, I'll do it again."

Ty's frown deepened. "Why? It wasn't anything serious."

"I can see you're gonna have to be set straight on a few things about women," Martha said. She stopped her bandaging to shake her finger at him. "A woman's place is at her man's side when he's sick or hurt. No matter how minor it is, that's where she wants to be and that's where a man needs her to be.''

He winced when Martha resumed wrapping the gauze around his arm. If he didn't know better, he'd swear she drew the bandage extra tight on purpose. ''I could have told her all about it once I got home.''

Martha shook her head. ''A wife doesn't want to hear somethin' like this secondhand. She wants to know what's goin' on right now.'' She took Ty's shirt from the hook on the back of the door and handed it to him. ''And that's her right. When she married you, Lexi promised to be at your side in sickness as well as in health, to face the good times with you as well as the bad.'' She shrugged. ''That's called trust, son. Without it, your marriage won't have a whisper in a whirlwind's chance of lastin'.''

Trust.

Ty felt his gut clench as he mulled over the word. He'd given Lexi his name, but that was about all he'd given her when they'd repeated their wedding vows. The day they were married, she'd gifted him with her trust just by placing her hands in his. But he hadn't believed her feelings for him could be strong enough to see past his parentage, hadn't had the faith that she would understand and love him anyway. He'd been wrong. She'd accepted his illegitimacy much easier than he had.

He closed his eyes and took a deep breath. Trust. One little word that could either make or break their marriage. And the one he had to accept, or risk losing Lexi forever.

Put that way, he really didn't see that he had any other choice. The time had come to lay his soul bare. He had to tell her what he'd kept hidden for so long, what had eventually driven him to temporarily leave Chicago.

He just hoped Lexi could accept it as easily as she had his parentage. And love him in spite of it all.

"There somethin' you gotta do before you go try to make things right with Lexi," Martha said, breaking into his thoughts.

Ty sighed heavily. "What's that, Martha?"

"You have to call Doc Fletcher. He says it's important and he needs to talk to you pronto."

Ty got out of Jeff's truck, then watched it disappear back down the long drive before turning to face the cabin. His arm ached, but the physical discomfort was nothing compared to the mixture of excitement and fear twisting his gut. He knew what he had to do, what he should have done when he'd had the nightmare a week ago.

Ty took a deep breath and slowly walked up the steps of the porch. He just hoped like hell it wasn't too late for them already.

"Lexi?" he called, entering the cabin.

Nothing.

His fear increased as he crossed the room and headed down the hall. What if he *was* too late?

Relief flooded him when he reached the door to the bedroom and heard Lexi's soft voice as she talked to their son.

"Lexi, honey, I—"

Ty stopped short at the sight of her clothes spread across the bed. The knot in his stomach tightened painfully. Walking over to the closet, he grabbed a clean shirt.

"Are you going somewhere?" he asked, careful to keep his voice even, in spite of the panic he felt.

He shrugged out of the bloody shirt and pulled on the clean one as he watched her finish changing Matthew's diaper. She placed the baby in the cradle before turning to face him.

That was when he saw the evidence of tears on her pale cheeks, the guarded look in her expressive green eyes. He hated that he'd been the cause of her anguish, hated to think that what he was about to tell her might cause her even more.

"I'm not the one who will be leaving," she said, her voice thick with tears. "But would it matter to you at all if one of us did?"

"Yes," he said, buttoning the soft flannel. He turned to face her. He didn't care anymore if he looked or sounded desperate. All that mattered was for Lexi to know the truth, to give him another chance. "I don't think I'd survive losing you, Lexi."

"Why?"

Ty rubbed at the tension building at the back of his neck. The look she'd given him spoke volumes. If he didn't tell her everything this time, he'd lose her for sure.

"We need to talk, Lexi."

"It's past time," she said, her voice reflecting her hurt.

Matthew began to make happy baby noises. The sound was one of the sweetest Ty had ever heard. A lump the size of his fist clogged his throat when he thought about how much he had at stake, what his admission might cost him.

"You look tired. Why don't you go into the living room and put your feet up?" he suggested, walking over to the cradle. He picked up Matthew, then turned to face her. "I'll join you as soon as I get the baby to sleep."

When Lexi nodded and left the room, Ty glanced down at his smiling son. "Wish me luck, little man."

Matthew gurgled and wrapped his tiny hand around Ty's finger.

"Thanks for the moral support," Ty said a moment before he closed his eyes against the emotions threatening to overwhelm him. "Daddy feels like he's about to take a blind leap off the side of the mountain."

Lexi watched Ty walk into the great room and, without a word, go over to the picture window. He stood for several long moments, staring at the mountains beyond. From his profile, she could tell he saw none of the scenic view.

"I didn't mean to hurt your feelings this afternoon at the clinic," he finally said. "I thought you'd be busy with the baby. I knew it wasn't serious and I couldn't see any reason to upset you."

"I'm not some hothouse flower, Ty. I don't need to be sheltered from reality." She stared at his broad shoulders, wishing he'd turn to face her. "I'm your wife. I'm supposed to know what's going on and be with you, not hear about these things later."

He gave her a short nod.

When he remained silent, she asked, "How is your arm?"

"It hurts like hell."

"Have you taken anything for it?"

He shook his head. "It's nothing I can't handle." He dragged in a ragged breath and turned to look at her. "Besides, I want to be sure I have a clear head for what I'm about to tell you."

Lexi's heart thudded against her ribs as she watched him straighten his wide shoulders, then turn to face her. She could tell that whatever he was about to say would be the most difficult thing he'd ever told anyone. Was he going to tell her he no longer wanted their marriage to work? Was he going to say goodbye?

"What would you like to know first?" he asked.

"Whatever you'd like to tell me," she answered quietly.

Ty shrugged. "I suppose we could start out with why I'm here in Dixie Ridge and not back in Chicago."

"Yes, Ty. We could."

She watched emotion cloud his clear blue gaze before he turned back to the window. "When we were together that night in your apartment, you talked about the beauty of the Smoky Mountains, how peaceful and laid-back the pace is here," he said, his voice even. "A few months ago I needed to get away for a while and decided to put out some feelers to see if there might be a community in the region in need of a doctor."

"About the same time Doc Fletcher was looking for someone to take over the clinic while he had surgery?" Lexi guessed.

Ty nodded. "He heard I was looking for a temporary position and got in touch with me."

"But I thought you liked your job."

"I did." He took a deep breath, then turned back to her. "But I've decided I can't continue as a trauma specialist any longer, Lexi."

"Why not? You're one of the best."

His face reflected his inner struggle, when he admitted, "I found, more times than I care to count, that I'm not." He jammed his hands into his jeans pockets, then shook his head. "The burnout rate for trauma specialists is high. I would have had to give it up eventually." He swallowed hard. "I think I could have handled it for a while longer, if it hadn't been for—"

She watched him squeeze his eyes shut on the memory. When he opened them, his bleak gaze was testament to how deeply he had been affected.

"Ty?"

"God, Lexi, I've seen too many kids die," he said, his voice raw with pent-up emotion. He took a deep shuddering breath. "I can't bear to stand over another gurney and have a child's eyes stare up at me with hope and trust, then watch them grow clouded and dull as life drains away."

Lexi bit her lower lip to keep it from trembling. She could tell it had taken a great deal of courage for him to admit what he viewed as a weakness, a failing. "I never realized what E.R. doctors have to deal with every day."

He sighed heavily. "I was arrogant enough to think I could handle it and remain detached." He shook his head. "I found out differently."

"I'm sure you saw some pretty horrendous things," she said gently. "Maybe after being away you'll feel differently when you go back, Ty."

"No. I've decided I can't go back to being a trauma specialist."

"I never—" Lexi's voice caught and she had to

pause a moment before she could continue. "I never realized how difficult it must be for you."

He ran a hand over his face as if to erase the dark memories. "Believe me, you wouldn't want to hear the ugly details."

Lexi felt her heart swell with love. Ty had tried to protect her from what he was going through—the tragic side of his profession—with his silence.

"You should have told me," she said firmly. "I've never been, nor will I ever be, someone who runs from the unpleasant aspects of life."

"It's a moot point now," he said, shrugging. He stared at her a moment before he added, "There's something else you need to know."

From the look on his face, Lexi knew his previous confession would pale in comparison to what he was about to tell her now.

He took a deep breath. "It happened the night we spent together," he said, his voice taking on a distant quality. "Nothing unusual for a weeknight. A couple of injuries from MVA's—car accidents. A knife wound." He paused. "Nothing major."

She could tell by his expression that whatever had taken place that evening had changed his life forever. "Ty?"

After several long minutes, he continued. "Everything was quiet, so I decided to go up to ICU to check on a patient I'd treated a few days earlier. I'd just stepped off the elevator when they paged me to get back down to E.R., stat."

He paused, his emotional pain obvious. The sight broke her heart.

"I arrived downstairs at the same time the ambulance pulled in," he finally said. "Everything was going our way. We had the kid out of the ambulance and wheeled into a treatment room in record time. He had a gunshot wound, but he was conscious and responsive. One of the nurses cut his shirt off, and I had just stepped up beside him when he went into cardiac arrest.''

She watched Ty walk over to the fireplace to brace both hands on the mantel as he struggled with the memory. When he finally turned to meet her gaze, his voice was suspiciously hoarse. ''My best just wasn't good enough.''

Tears flooded her eyes at the sight of his pain. ''Oh, Ty. I'm so sorry.''

He nodded. ''When I went out to talk to his family, the boy's brother lost it and pulled a gun.'' Ty took another deep breath before he could continue, his voice raw with emotion. ''It was clear the kid was high, but there was no reasoning with him. Hell, I doubt he even heard me. He was waving the gun, threatening to shoot everyone in the waiting area. But when he pointed it at a little girl, I knew I had to do something. I jumped him and while I tried to get the gun, it went off. He was hit.'' His big body shuddered. ''We started working on him right there on the waiting room floor.'' He closed his eyes. When he opened them, his gaze begged for her understanding. ''I swear, Lexi, I did everything I could to save him. But his mother started screaming that I'd let her son die on purpose.''

She wished she could make things easier for him. But she sensed there wasn't anything she could say or do to take away the memory of that fateful night.

''She was overwrought,'' Lexi said gently. ''She didn't know what—''

Lexi winced at the tortured look that crossed his face. "The woman knew exactly what she was accusing me of," he said bleakly.

Despite the warmth from the fire she'd built to chase away the early evening chill, Lexi shivered. Tears streaming down her cheeks, she left the couch to walk over to him.

She put her arms around his stiff shoulders. "How do you know she meant what she said?"

"Even after the investigation cleared me of any wrongdoing, she continued to pursue me through the media." He swallowed hard. "For nine months she called into radio talk shows, sent editorials to the newspapers, and even called the hospital administrator daily to demand that I be fired. When she didn't give up, the administration suggested I take a leave of absence and drop out of sight to see if that would stop her."

"Oh, Ty." Lexi felt his pain as deeply as if it were her own. There wasn't a doubt in her mind of his innocence. Putting her arms around him again, she held him close. "You didn't mean for it to happen. The police cleared you of any charges."

His gaze intense, he took a deep shuddering breath and placed his hands on her shoulders. "Can you love a man who's killed another human being, Lexi?"

"Ty, it wasn't your fault," she said, placing her hand on his cheek. "You could have just as easily been the one shot."

"Yes, but—"

"I know you, Ty. You would never harm someone intentionally." Taking his hands in hers, she asked, "How many lives have these hands saved, Ty? How many people are alive today because you were on duty when they arrived in the E.R.?"

When he shrugged, she looked directly into his deep blue eyes. "It was an accident, Ty. You're no more at fault in that boy's death than he was himself. You have to forgive yourself."

"I've learned to live with what happened," he said, his tone guarded. "But I thought you might not—"

"You know what your problem is, Dr. Braden?" she interrupted. "You think too much."

The disbelieving frown on his handsome face made her realize how deeply his doubts ran.

She walked over to the door and turned the lock. "It looks like I'll just have to show you that I mean what I'm saying."

Ty watched Lexi cross the room to stand before him. His arm ached, but he paid little attention to the pain as he took her into his embrace. He'd seen compassion in her eyes, but none of the accusations he'd feared. Hope began to flare as he stared down at her.

"What did you have in mind, Mrs. Braden?"

"You'll see," she said, pulling away from him. She took him by the hand and led him over to the fireplace. Reaching up, she pushed the top button of his shirt through the button hole.

"I just put this on."

"I know."

"And you're going to take it off?"

"Um-hmm." She loosened the rest of the buttons and carefully removed the garment from his injured arm. "I can't show you what country lovin' is all about if I don't."

"I didn't realize there was a difference between

city and country loving,'' he said, his body responding to her soft touch.

''Oh, yes.'' She gave him a look that made his mouth go dry. ''There's a *big* difference.''

Ty allowed her to pull him down onto the braided rug in front of the hearth. ''Do you think I'll like it?''

''Absolutely.''

Feeling more free than he'd ever felt in his life, he found he was more than ready to put into words what he'd known from the moment they met. ''I love you, Lexi. I've always loved you.''

She gave him a smile that sent his blood pressure skyrocketing. ''Now I'm going to prove to you once and for all that *I* love you. I'm going to fulfill one of your fantasies, and by the time I'm finished, there won't be a doubt left about my believing you. Or the way I feel about you.''

To Ty's utter amazement, she did just that.

Lexi smiled up at Ty when he handed Matthew to her. Guiding her breast to the baby's searching mouth, she asked, ''Do you think you could get used to country lovin', Dr. Braden?''

''Definitely.'' He grinned as he settled beside Lexi on the big leather couch, then wrapped his arms around her and their son. ''I'm finding I like all aspects of country life. Especially the loving.''

''I'm glad to hear that,'' she said, her tone leaving no doubt in his mind about her contentment.

Ty kissed the top of her head. ''How did you know I fantasized about making love to you in front of the fireplace?''

She smiled. ''I saw the look on your face the first

day you stopped by here. You couldn't take your eyes off it.''

''I was pretty transparent, huh?''

''As a pane of glass.''

They were silent for a time as Ty watched his son nursing at her breast. He felt like the luckiest man alive.

''Will you set up a private practice when we return to Chicago?'' Lexi asked.

He stared at her intently. ''You'd go back with me?''

''Of course.'' She gave him a reassuring smile. ''A family should be together.''

He kissed the top of her head. She was willing to go with him, even though he knew raising their son in the city wasn't what she wanted to do. ''We're not going back.''

Her expression reflecting her happiness, she pulled back to stare at him. ''We're staying here?''

Ty nodded. ''After you left the clinic this afternoon, Martha gave me a message to call Dr. Fletcher. Seems he's enjoyed being home so much, he's decided to retire. He's asked me to take over his practice here in Dixie Ridge.''

''Do you like living here, Ty?'' she asked cautiously. ''It's a lot different than you're used to.''

He chuckled. ''I have to admit, I thought places like this only existed on television or in the movies.''

''Culture shock?'' she asked, laughing with him.

He nodded. ''Some of the quirky neighbors and their odd customs take a while to get used to. But I'm finding I like being part of this community. And I like being a country doctor.''

Lexi smiled. "Good. This is where I want to raise our children."

Ty felt some of his anxiety return. "You don't want to return to a career in radio somewhere?"

Lexi leaned back to look at him. "Would it bother you if I said yes?"

"No," he answered honestly. "I'd never stand in your way or ask you to give it up. But I'd like to remain in the area, if possible. Do you think we could make a long-distance relationship work if you did?"

She used her finger to ease the frown lines on his forehead. "It's not an issue. I'm perfectly happy being a wife and mother. But if I do decide I want to resume my career, I can take a part-time job with the local station."

He gazed at her for several long moments. "Are you sure?" he asked again. He didn't want her to feel pressured.

"Alexis Madison doesn't exist anymore. All that's left is plain old Lexi Braden, super wife and mother."

Ty laughed. "There never has been, nor will there ever be, anything plain about you, honey." His smile faded as he asked, "But what about the clothes on the bed? When I came home, I thought—"

"There you go again," Lexi said, grinning. "I warned you about thinking too much. I was sorting out some maternity tops for Freddie." She kissed his cheek. "Get used to it, Ty. I'm not going anywhere. You have me for better or for worse, for as long as we both shall live. I want nothing more than to be your wife and the mother of a whole house full of Braden children."

"A house full?"

"Oh, yes." Lexi grinned. "But I'll need help."

Ty grinned back. "What kind of help, Mrs. Braden?"

"Someone is going to have to help me get that house full of children," she reasoned. "Do you think you're up to the task?"

Feeling all the joy and wonder he'd never dreamed would be his to treasure, Ty laughed. "I'll give it my best shot."

"I'd like for Matthew to have a baby brother or sister in a year or two," Lexi said, snuggling close.

"I think that sounds like a good idea." Ty placed his finger close to his son's hand. "What do you think, little man? Would you like to have a little brother or sister?"

Matthew wrapped his hand around Ty's finger, smiled a toothless baby smile and gurgled his agreement.

Epilogue

"**J**eff, if you don't shut off that video camera, I'm gonna have to hurt you," Freddie said through clenched teeth.

"Sweetheart, I thought—"

"Come on, Freddie," Lexi urged. "Forget about him. Take a deep cleansing breath. Now pant, pant, blow. Pant, pant, blow."

Freddie did as she was told, but when the contraction ended, she glared up at Lexi. "I've changed my mind. I don't want to do this anymore."

"Too late now," Lexi said, her smile sympathetic as she gazed down at her red-faced sister-in-law.

Freddie had been in labor for the past eight hours and Lexi knew she had to be exhausted. Sponging the perspiration from Freddie's brow, she offered, "If it's any consolation, you'll forget all about the pain as soon as you see your baby."

"Maybe I will, but I'm gonna make sure Jeff doesn't," Freddie shot back, turning her deep scowl on her husband. She suddenly scrunched her face and gripped Lexi's hand. "Oh, no. Here comes another one."

Lexi coached Freddie through the pain, then glanced up at Ty as he positioned himself at the end of the bed. "It won't be much longer."

Smiling, Ty shook his head. "You can start pushing with the next contraction, Freddie."

"Finally," Freddie groaned. "I didn't think I'd ever get to the end of this."

"You're doin' fine," Martha called from the doorway. She turned her attention to Ty. "I've got everything ready for when the baby pops out, Doc."

"Good. We're almost there," Ty said. "The head is crowning now."

Lexi supported her shoulders as Freddie squeezed her eyes shut and pushed with all her might.

"Oh, Lord," Jeff groaned.

Lexi watched her brother lay the video camera on the bedside table. He looked suspiciously green. "Are you going to be all right, Jeff?"

He nodded a moment before he hit the floor in a dead faint.

"The bigger they are, the harder they fall," Martha said, stepping over Jeff to stand beside Ty.

Lexi felt tears of joy burn the backs of her eyes as she watched Ty place his hands beneath the emerging infant and finish the delivery. "You have a little boy, Freddie," she said, hugging her sister-in-law. She glanced across the bedroom to where her brother lay sprawled on the floor. "I just wish Jeff hadn't missed it."

Freddie laughed as she looked over at her husband. "When he wakes up, tell him *he* had the baby. He'll never know the difference."

Ty watched Miss Eunice's car disappear around the bend of the drive in the predawn light. They'd called on the woman several times recently to baby-sit Matthew. Fortunately, the kindhearted shop owner didn't mind the odd hours he and Lexi were forced to keep.

He smiled. So much had changed in the past few months.

When he made the decision to start the home delivery program, Granny Applegate had given him her heartfelt blessings, retired from midwifery and moved to the warmer climate of southern Florida to be near her daughter's family. Martha had readily agreed to assist him, taking care of the babies once they were born. And Lexi had fallen into the role of paternal counselor and delivery coach when the father was too nervous or, like Jeff, passed out on the floor.

They had formed a very efficient home delivery team. And just in time, too. They'd delivered four babies this week alone; Mary Ann and Jake Sanders's new daughter, Helen McKinney's twins and now Jeff and Freddie's son.

His introspection stopped suddenly when a pair of arms wrapped around his waist from behind.

"What are you thinking about?" Lexi asked, resting her head against his back.

Ty turned to take her into his arms. "I was thinking what a great team we make." He gave her a kiss that left them both breathless. "Is Matthew still asleep?"

Lexi nodded. "I think he'll sleep until it's time to go visit Dempsey."

Luckily Ty had been able to convince Carl that Dempsey would be much happier with the other pigs in Carl's recently expanded hog business. Ty shook his head. He still couldn't believe that he, Lexi and Matthew made a weekly habit of visiting the now full-grown hog.

Ty abandoned all thought of Dempsey when Lexi nuzzled his neck and whispered close to his ear, "I thought we might take a nap before we leave."

"That would be very nice," he agreed, his body responding to the thought of holding his wife, loving her. When Lexi yawned, he kissed the top of her head. "I think you'd better take that nap alone. You've been working too hard."

She shook her head. "Not really. When I first got pregnant with Matthew, I felt this way."

Ty grinned. "Are you trying to tell me you're—"

Lexi nodded, her smile radiant. "I think you're going to be a daddy again, Ty."

"I love you," he said, holding her close.

"And I love you."

They watched the sun rise over the tops of the misty mountains, the light painting the trees with the colors of morning.

"Let's go inside," he whispered. "We have some celebrating to do."

Lexi gave him a look that raised his temperature several degrees. "What kind of celebration did you have in mind, Dr. Braden?"

"Country style, Mrs. Braden." Grinning, he took her hand in his and led her into the cabin. "Country style suits me just fine."

* * * * *

SILHOUETTE® MAKES YOU A STAR!

Feel like a star with Silhouette.

We will fly you and a guest to New York City for an exciting weekend stay at a glamorous 5-star hotel. Experience a refreshing day at one of New York's trendiest spas and have your photo taken by a professional. Plus, receive $1,000 U.S. spending money!

Flowers...long walks...dinner for two... how does Silhouette Books make romance come alive for you?

Send us a script, with 500 words or less, along with visuals (only drawings, magazine cutouts or photographs or combination thereof). Show us how Silhouette Makes Your Love Come Alive. Be creative and have fun. No purchase necessary. All entries must be clearly marked with your name, address and telephone number. All entries will become property of Silhouette and are not returnable. **Contest closes September 28, 2001.**

Please send your entry to: **Silhouette Makes You a Star!**

In U.S.A.
P.O. Box 9069
Buffalo, NY, 14269-9069

In Canada
P.O. Box 637
Fort Erie, ON, L2A 5X3

Look for contest details on the next page, by visiting www.eHarlequin.com or request a copy by sending a self-addressed envelope to the applicable address above. Contest open to Canadian and U.S. residents who are 18 or over. Void where prohibited.

Silhouette®
Where love comes alive™

Our lucky winner's photo will appear in a Silhouette ad. Join the fun!

SRMYAS1

HARLEQUIN "SILHOUETTE MAKES YOU A STAR!" CONTEST 1308
OFFICIAL RULES
NO PURCHASE NECESSARY TO ENTER

1. To enter, follow directions published in the offer to which you are responding. Contest begins June 1, 2001, and ends on September 28, 2001. Entries must be postmarked by September 28, 2001, and received by October 5, 2001. Enter by hand-printing (or typing) on an 8 ½" x 11" piece of paper your name, address (including zip code), contest number/name and attaching a script containing 500 words or less, <u>along with drawings, photographs or magazine cutouts, or combinations thereof</u> (i.e., collage) <u>on no larger than 9" x 12"</u> piece of paper, describing how the <u>Silhouette books make romance come alive for you.</u> Mail via first-class mail to: Harlequin "Silhouette Makes You a Star!" Contest 1308, (in the U.S.) P.O. Box 9069, Buffalo, NY 14269-9069, (in Canada) P.O. Box 637, Fort Erie, Ontario, Canada L2A 5X3. Limit one entry per person, household or organization.

2. Contests will be judged by a panel of members of the Harlequin editorial, marketing and public relations staff. Fifty percent of criteria will be judged against script and fifty percent will be judged against drawing, photographs and/or magazine cutouts. Judging criteria will be based on the following:

   - Sincerity—25%
   - Originality and Creativity—50%
   - Emotionally Compelling—25%

   In the event of a tie, duplicate prizes will be awarded. Decisions of the judges are final.

3. All entries become the property of Torstar Corp. and may be used for future promotional purposes. Entries will not be returned. No responsibility is assumed for lost, late, illegible, incomplete, inaccurate, nondelivered or misdirected mail.

4. Contest open only to residents of the U.S. (except Puerto Rico) and Canada who are 18 years of age or older, and is void wherever prohibited by law; all applicable laws and regulations apply. Any litigation within the Province of Quebec respecting the conduct or organization of a publicity contest may be submitted to the Régie des alcools, des courses et des jeux for a ruling. Any litigation respecting the awarding of a prize may be submitted to the Régie des alcools, des courses et des jeux only for the purpose of helping the parties reach a settlement. Employees and immediate family members of Torstar Corp. and D. L. Blair, Inc., their affiliates, subsidiaries and all other agencies, entities and persons connected with the use, marketing or conduct of this contest are not eligible to enter. Taxes on prizes are the sole responsibility of the winner. Acceptance of any prize offered constitutes permission to use winner's name, photograph or other likeness for the purposes of advertising, trade and promotion on behalf of Torstar Corp., its affiliates and subsidiaries without further compensation to the winner, unless prohibited by law.

5. Winner will be determined no later than November 30, 2001, and will be notified by mail. Winner will be required to sign and return an Affidavit of Eligibility/Release of Liability/Publicity Release form within 15 days after winner notification. Noncompliance within that time period may result in disqualification and an alternative winner may be selected. All travelers must execute a Release of Liability prior to ticketing and must possess required travel documents (e.g., passport, photo ID) where applicable. Trip must be booked by December 31, 2001, and completed within one year of notification. No substitution of prize permitted by winner. Torstar Corp. and D. L. Blair, Inc., their parents, affiliates and subsidiaries are not responsible for errors in printing of contest, entries and/or game pieces. In the event of printing or other errors that may result in unintended prize values or duplication of prizes, all affected game pieces or entries shall be null and void. **Purchase or acceptance of a product offer does not improve your chances of winning.**

6. Prizes: (1) Grand Prize—A 2-night/3-day trip for two (2) to New York City, including round-trip coach air transportation nearest winner's home and hotel accommodations (double occupancy) at The Plaza Hotel, a glamorous afternoon makeover at <u>a trendy New York spa</u>, $1,000 in U.S. spending money and an opportunity to <u>have a professional photo taken and appear in a Silhouette advertisement</u> (approximate retail value: $7,000). (10) Ten Runner-Up Prizes of gift packages (retail value $50 ea.). Prizes consist of only those items listed as part of the prize. Limit one prize per person. Prize is valued in U.S. currency.

7. For the name of the winner (available after December 31, 2001) send a self-addressed, stamped envelope to: Harlequin "Silhouette Makes You a Star!" Contest 1197 Winners, P.O. Box 4200 Blair, NE 68009-4200 or you may access the www.eHarlequin.com Web site through February 28, 2002.

Contest sponsored by Torstar Corp., P.O. Box 9042, Buffalo, NY 14269-9042.

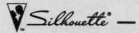